MW00781430

I'll See You
In My Dreams

By

Doreen G. Kimmel

ℰ
Eloquent Books
New York, New York

Eloquent Books
An imprint of AEG Publishing Group
845 Third Avenue, 6th Floor - 6016
New York, NY 10022
www.eloquentbooks.com

ISBN: 978-1-934925-47-8
SKU: 1-934925-47-0

Printed in the United States of America

Book Design: Roger Hayes

DEDICATION

To Mom and Dad—the memories of your love and nurturing remain in my heart. Now I have two angels watching over me. You are with me always in my dreams. 'Till we meet again . . .

Make yourself familiar with the angels, and behold them frequently in spirit; for without being seen, they are present with you.

—St. Francis de Sales

Acknowledgements

I would like to acknowledge my husband Allan for his patience and encouragement for the past year that he steadfastly remained at my side while I wrote this story of my parents through teary eyes.

Chapter 1

Every man has his own idea of what "living and loving" means to him. For me, it all really started in 1927 when I was nine years old. Mid-September on Mulberry Street was no different to me than any other time of the year ever since I could remember. "Living" was sharing a tenement apartment with "loving" parents who had migrated from Sicily in 1912, and six brothers who looked as scrawny and poorly clothed as me. Our papa worked hard in construction and brought home the bread. And mama, well she tried hard, but having babies almost every year since 1913 and losing three infants to the flu was breaking her down year after year. We older boys pitched in by quitting school and getting work wherever work was available. I was delivering donuts from Maggio's Bakery twice a week, sweeping the barroom floor at Flynn's Taproom six days a week and spending four days at the public library. I loved to read. The donut deliveries were hard, especially during the long hot summer days. But I enjoyed the aromas coming from the apartments and the old world congeniality of the Italian immigrants. It sure beat the smell of the beer soaked sawdust on the floor of the bar.

Ah, but getting back to the "loving" part of my life. This was the year when I discovered "love" for the first time. One fortuitous day in mid-September changed my life forever. It was the second day of the San Gennaro Feast that was

5

celebrated every year in honor of Saint Gennaro. Well that was what it was supposed to be, and to all good Catholics it was. The truth is that all Italians (Sicilians, Calabrese, Neapolitans, and so on) had this time to not only celebrate San Gennaro but to perpetuate the memories of the country of their birth and the families they left behind. All of the Little Italy residents gathered in the street to meet with family and friends. They huddled in small groups and spoke of the oppression and failing economy that had driven them to leave their country in the hope of finding a fruitful life in America. But now was the time to kick up their heels and celebrate. There was singing, Old-World entertainers, and dancing to the tarantella. The statue of San Gennaro and the shrines and relics of this saint were paraded through the street, which was renamed Via San Gennaro for the ten-day feast.

As the statue of San Gennaro went past me I glanced up at one of the buildings and was almost blinded by what I saw. A vision appeared in the form of an angel. She had long golden hair with a halo shining above her head. A bright white gown flowed over her body and white feathery wings fluttered on her back. Her face was all aglow and her cheeks and tiny lips were pink. She was exquisite. For a moment I thought she had looked right at me and smiled. My legs felt weak and began to buckle under me. I had to sit on the nearest stoop and just glory in my fortune. I was about to thank God for this vision when what I saw next brought me back to reality. There were thin wires strapped around her waist, going around to her back and attached to one of the tenements. "My God, she's just a little girl." And God was the right one to talk to because he had created the most beautiful girl I had ever seen. She was truly an angel. I was spellbound. I had become oblivious to everything around me. I closed my eyes for what seemed like only a moment. When I looked up again she was gone. Where she could have disappeared to was beyond me. I looked everywhere possible but there was no sign of her. Had I been dreaming? It must have been my imagination. Angels never appeared to me before.

6

Chapter 2

Besides she was really just a little girl. Wasn't she?

All I could think of that night was the angel that I would probably never see again. Just the thought of her filled me with a love I had never experienced before. I started for home and turned once more to see if she had returned. She was gone, my angel.

The feast was over and I was delivering my donuts as usual. It was one of those Indian summer days of September that brings back the last, blistering hot days of a summer that should be gone by now. Sweaty wet hair was clinging to my forehead and my shoulder was aching from the weight of the metal tray laden with fresh donuts. The building I had just entered was smothering hot. The worn tile steps I climbed to each landing were a memory of happier days long since gone. Italian immigrants, living their new lives, were behind the heavy metal doors. I admired these people for their values and their will to better the lives of their children. But today was just another day for me. I was hot and tired and grateful that this building on Elizabeth Street was the last of my deliveries. My delivery route covered Mulberry Street, Mott Street, and Elizabeth Street between Prince Street and Houston Street. By the time I got to Elizabeth Street I was ready to drop. I couldn't wait to finish up and maybe go for a swim at the docks with my brothers.

I was down to a dozen donuts when I came to the last door on my route. As the door opened I froze on the spot. Sun from the window inside the apartment was casting its golden rays on the angel of my dreams. This couldn't be happening. I must have heat stroke or something.

I stood there with my mouth wide open and nothing coming out, not even my breath. I don't know how long I stood there looking like an idiot. Through the cloudy mist in my head I heard her speak. "Hi Joe," Holy cow, she knows my name.

My voice finally came to me as I croaked "Want any donuts today?"

She spoke again "Sure, we'll take six please."

I almost dropped the tray as I pushed it forward for her to pick out the ones she wanted, and nearly shoved the tray in her face. Goofy. She took her donuts and as she was getting ready to go back into the apartment, I bleated out "How do you know my name?"

She told me, " My name is Rose, and me and my sisters have seen you and your brothers at the Chrystie Street Park a few times." She smiled and closed the door. I stood against the wall almost paralyzed for a few minutes, and finally found my legs and went slowly down the stairs. This was my first miracle. My angel appeared before me once more and actually knew me. I know it sounds crazy but deep in my heart I felt the surge of love. The question at this point is, what does a nine-year-old boy know of love? Nine years old? No way. Impossible. But believe it or not I knew and have known from that day on that I was hopelessly in love with Rose. My angel forever.

Somehow I made it to the bakery, dropped off the donut tray and money, and found myself sitting on the dock just gazing at the water. The sun glistening on the river formed sparkling images of angels, and among them was my angel. Her golden hair flowed over the slight waves and her blue eyes twinkled as the movement of the water swirled back and forth.

A sudden slap at the back of my head brought me to my senses. "Hey kid, where've you been?" It was my big brother Sam and a couple of our friends.

"I've been right here." I said. "Why?"

Sam laughed, "You were not right here. You look like you've been on another planet. What were you dreaming about, some girl?"

Some girl? No, my angel, I thought. "I'll see you in my dreams." And I did.

Summer turned to fall, fall turned to winter. It was all natural and predictable. But the days always turned to Sunday for me. That was the day I lived for. After Sunday mass at the Old St. Patrick's church my brothers Sam, Mike and I rushed to the Chrystie Street Park. I told them it was because I liked the country atmosphere and they laughed because they knew it was my chance to see Rose. So what, let them laugh. It was true anyway. Rose and her sisters were always there every Sunday no matter what the weather was like. We sat on the swings and talked for hours. Did we talk about Kid stuff? Did we talk about School stuff? Was it Puppy Love? Let them say what they wanted. We were there because we liked each other. I became her best friend and she became mine. Most of the time her sisters and my brothers played stickball or tag. We never touched or spoke of more than friendship. After all, we were just kids who enjoyed each other's company. Right? By the end of the year I was walking on air and was the happiest I had ever been. "Loving"? Oh I was doing that all right. "Living"? Oh yeah, I was enjoying that too. But the man up there had other plans for me and Rose.

9

Chapter 3

My family was crumbling right before my eyes and I never saw it coming. Mama had been more and more depressed all year. She was sick a lot with the flu and was in and out of the hospital a couple of times. Neighbors and friends helped her with our baby brother who was only six months old. She constantly complained of pain, and at times her headaches were so bad that her eyes would roll and sometimes she seemed not to know where she was. Mama never tried to learn to speak English, so when she saw the doctors they had no way of knowing what she was saying about her pain and headaches. Pop didn't make things any better for her either. Most of the time he wasn't even around.

And when he was home, we kids would walk in on him scolding mama for not taking proper care of the baby and herself. We heard him tell her she was no good to anyone any more. Her days became more and more unbearable for her and she cried all the time. When I was alone with her one day, I asked her why she cried all the time. She sobbed that her life was not here but back in Palermo where her mother and five brothers and sisters needed her. Pop walked in and said that she was talking foolish. He said her head was not right. She accused him of fooling around and he said, "See, She's become crazy."

Somehow the Child Welfare Organization stepped in and our lives were turned upside down in one fell swoop of the government. Mama was being sent to a hospital. We had no idea where that was and why she was going to be taken away in an ambulance. All we knew was that some people came for me and my six brothers, told us to say goodbye to papa and mama and that these people were going to help us. And that was that.

One day we were a family, and the next day mama was going one away, papa was going who knows where, and we were being hauled off to the unknown. There was no time for goodbyes or explanations to friends and neighbors; we just had to hurry up and get moving. There were a lot of questions and crying from the seven of us. We all looked questioningly to Papa but he just turned and walked away. There were no tears, no hugs, and no promises of salvation. Nothing. He just shrugged off an apparent burden and didn't seem to even care. This was a nightmare. Mama was crying and calling to us in Italian. We tried running to her, but the ambulance people had no idea what she was saying, held us back, and sped away. Just like that our parents were gone. Our lives were never the same again.

Chapter 4

The Catholic Home Bureau For Dependent Children shuffled us around until we were separated and put in what they called the home. It felt more like a prison to us. We found out much later that it was actually an orphanage. Sam and I were put into a cold, long room with twenty beds. Mike and Lou were with boys their own age, and Tony and Phil were in the infant quarters. We had no idea where Angelo was.

I was terrified the first night in the home. When we were ordered to bed and the lights went out, I started shaking all over. Sam came to me and climbed into bed with me. "Listen Joey, I know you're scared. So am I. This is probably a mistake anyway. You'll see, we'll be out of here before you know it." Sam was trying to be reassuring, but I couldn't help but worry about our brothers.

"Sam, the little guys are sure to be more frightened than you and me. They've always depended on us. Now who do they have? They are surrounded by strangers. They must be scared to death."

"Joey, sure we always took care of them before this happened, and we will be together again."

"But Sam, what if they think we deserted them? They might hate us right now. They're so young and they must be totally confused. Will we ever be a family again?"

Poor Sam, he was confused too. I knew that whatever happened to us, that we would never forget our brothers or our parents.

Sam and I tried to keep in touch with the little guys as best we could. When we did get to see them it was through fences that we couldn't climb. We only saw Mike and Lou. None of us knew where they were keeping our youngest brothers. Sometimes Mike and Lou were able to sneak close to the fence and tell us how they were doing. They weren't doing well at all. They were cold and hungry most of the time and didn't know yet how to get to our little guys.

Sam and I came up with a plan. Every Monday, when we were all allowed to play outdoors, we would pick potatoes and stuff them in our coats. As soon as the coast was clear, we would meet Mike and Lou at the fence and throw the potatoes over for them. We would also stuff our bread in our shirts, and throw that over too. As often as we could, and with the help of some of the guys in our section we would all hide mittens, socks, and shirts in our under drawers to squeeze through the fence for our brothers. We never got caught, and we never saw the three little guys again.

During the second year Mike was sent to our side of the home, and Lou was alone. We still hadn't seen or heard anything about Angelo, Tony, and Phil. We gave up on ever seeing Pop again because for some reason he had never come to see us. As for mama, nobody would tell us anything. Our days were filled with anxiety over our mama and our brothers. Our nights were no better. All we could do was pray that our family was alive, and that we would see each other again. The nights were the worst. Everybody was cold and very hungry. Muffled crying could be heard all around us. None of these kids would ever admit that they cried or how lonely and unhappy they were. Our only consolation was that we were all in the same boat, and we would help each other in every way possible. I guess Sam, Mike and I were the luckiest of all because we still had each other and at least we were getting some schooling again. That was the only thing I looked forward to. I wanted to learn as much as possible.

Chapter 5

Someday, I would be out of the home and I wanted a better life for myself and my angel, Rose. We would meet again. Of that I was certain. Getting free of the home was the key. Once out, we would find our mama and our brothers.

The only females we saw were the nuns. Dressed in their habits and their rosaries around their hips, they gave a saintly impression. They spoke in whispers to each other and to the few priests who were also there. But, in the room that they called the classroom, their voices boomed at us and the long wooden ruler was always ready for action. Every once in a while, one of the guys would act out and when the priest was called in, we wouldn't see that guy for three days. When he did come back he was all holier than thou.

One night when we were all in bed and the lights were out, Sam told Mike and me that he had a plan for us. We were to listen to him and swear that we would do exactly as he said. He was now the head of our family no matter where we were, and especially in this place. We were to do as we were told by the nuns and priests, or else he would give us more than a smack or two. If we didn't abide by his wishes for us to stay out of trouble, the day would come when we would be released from this place, and he would turn his back on us too. When he was finished, we held hands and swore before God "No one will ever take us away from each other again."

By the fourth year, we were handed a bushel of misery. Sam was old enough to be sent home, wherever that was, and to fend for himself. Me, Mike and now Lou were together and we finally had some news about Angelo. Sam had gone back to Little Italy and asked around the neighborhood for as much information about our family as possible. Most of what he heard was rumor. The only positive news he had gathered was that Angelo had been adopted during his first few months at the home. We were all in shock. How could any of us be adopted if we still had parents? Unless our parents had given us up. But mama was still in the hospital, and she would never willingly desert us. Then it was Pop.

He had gone away and nobody had seen nor heard from him anymore. This whole new idea of possible adoption put a bigger fear in us. We always assumed that once mama was better, that she and Pop would come for us. We were abandoned. There was no hope of ever going home now, and could it be possible that Tony and Phil were adopted too? We might never see any of them again. Or even each other, since we would be released at different times. Sam said not to worry because we were too old for anyone to want to adopt us, and besides we were an ugly bunch. He was going to get a good job in construction, stash away some money, and get a nice apartment. When we got out we would have a home to go to and he would take care of us. He was really the papa now and we thanked God for that. In three more years we would all be together again and then we would start our search for our three youngest brothers. Sam promised that one day we seven brothers would be together once again and for always.

Chapter 6

Time goes faster when you have a dream to follow, and before I knew it I was home with Sam. He got me a job working with him and we started getting things set up for Mike and Lou. We were so busy working and visiting our brothers that nothing else seemed to matter. One day Sam came home from work and said that he had been talking to some guys about a new work program that the New York Governor, Franklin Delano Roosevelt was trying to start for the New York unemployed. His plans had to be put on hold because he was elected to take over the office of the president of the United States the next year. The word was, the possibility for guys like me and Sam to make a good living and support a family looked pretty good with this new president. It sounded great.

Since 1927, Rose had never been more than a dream away. Now that I was back home I had been to Rose's apartment a couple of times before I finally found out that I might never see her again. Her family had moved to someplace in Brooklyn. I was sad to hear that Rose's father had died from a landslide on one of the construction jobs he was working. I could not imagine the horror and sorrow her family had gone through at losing the man they all loved. Death is bad enough but being buried alive is a horrendous way to go. I prayed that Rose, her mother and her siblings were rebuilding their lives and had

16

found happiness again. Apparently, Rose's mother remarried a couple of years later to a widower with three children. That's why they left Little Italy, they needed a bigger place to live in with so many children. But who was the new father and where in Brooklyn were they? I was in a state of despair at that point. My angel was nowhere to be found. She was gone from me forever.

Chapter 7

Somehow, someday I will find her again. I just had to make it my business to keep searching for her. Please little angel, don't forget me.

When 1933 came around, Sam, Mike, Lou and myself were finally together and the world was changing. President FDR set up The Civilian Conservation Corps in an effort to use the resources of young men who needed employment in his fight against soil erosion and declining timber in the land. Mike and Lou were too young to sign up for the CCC camps so Sam and I set them up with jobs and an apartment before we both left for the camps. A whole new world opened up for us. We were transported to the Winooski River Valley in Vermont by the Army. Suddenly we were in a new life, surrounded by trees and the invigorating beauty of forests and rivers. We lived in tents, it wasn't bad at all. They gave us uniforms to wear and we were joined by young guys from all across America. We worked hard building roads, cutting down trees and stringing up telephone lines. We ate good food and became stronger and healthier. Part of our salaries was sent home for our brothers and most of the rest of our money went into savings accounts. This was "living."

There were educational advisors who trained the uneducated and unskilled. My first glimpse of what I wanted for my future was when I met one of them. Mr. Ludlam. He was offering his skills as a surveyor and builder. For some reason we took a liking to each other and my destiny began to unfold. Mr. Ludlam had become my friend and mentor for the next forty years. He was my salvation. He taught me all about surveying and how to read and make construction blueprints. I guess I surprised him when he saw how quickly I learned despite my short time of formal schooling. The time spent in the library when I was so young panned out for me. Sam, in the meantime, had also found his future, in being an electrician. He loved everything about working with wires and lighting up the world. Thank you President Roosevelt and Mr. Ludlam. I will be going home a man with hopes and dreams that can be fulfilled. We spent two years in the CCC camps, and then it was time to go home.

Home! We went home healthier, stronger, smarter, and with broadening horizons. Hello New York. Hello Little Italy. I was ready and willing to conquer my destiny. But hold on. Isn't Rose a part of my destiny? Can I find her? Yes, if I have to search forever I will find my angel again. I had a new life to share now and all I needed was my love at my side.

Chapter 8

I started wandering the streets after work in an effort to find anyone who might know where Rose and her family had gone. I found nothing. It was as though the earth had swallowed up her whole family. I finally gave up one weekend and went back to Old St Patrick's Church to pray for an answer. It felt good to be back in that old church with all the happy memories. But I still felt unfulfilled and downhearted. I decided to go to the Chrystie Street Park and just sit on the swing and remember how beautiful life had been for that short period in my life. The park was empty and kind of rundown but the swings were still there. They were a little rickety and looked like they were about ready to collapse. *What the heck,* I thought. *If I fall, I fall.* Surprise, surprise the swing held up. I sat there staring at the dirt beneath my feet, and lost in memories, when I heard voices.

A young woman with her back to me was saying something very quietly to a skinny guy who looked vaguely familiar. His voice was getting louder as he talked to her and I could hear him telling her that he had been longing to meet her after seeing her here in this park a few weeks before. She replied to him, again in a low tone, something that seemed to infuriate him. The next thing I knew he was holding her arms and she was struggling to get away from him. She stopped struggling and kicked him instead. I had a pretty good idea where she kicked him because

23

he quickly doubled over and started cursing her. She told him in a voice not as timid as before to "get lost." He came at her with his hand coming up and I rushed him. One hard shove and he was on his butt. I told him "You better take her advice and get lost." He hissed at me like a snake and slithered away. I just laughed and turned to face his intended victim.

I heard her cry out towards the retreating bonehead. "You wannabe crooner, go back to New Jersey."

I turned to face her and was awed by her beauty. "No wonder he's crazy about you. You're beautiful." She looked at me in such astonishment that I thought that she must have thought that I was another masher. "I'm sorry, I meant no offense."

She looked at me with the biggest blue eyes I'd ever seen and said "No offense taken Joe. You are Joe aren't you?"

Oh dear God it can't be. It seemed like years before as my voice squeaked out "Yes, but?"

She touched my hand and said, "I've never forgotten our friendship, have you?"

I told her I'd been looking for her all year, and thought I'd never see her again. She laughed and told me that she worked at a hat factory on Orchard Street and that she stopped by the park often, hoping to find me. We hugged and both laughed at the mysteries of life. We were like kids again remembering the happiness we had shared years ago. After a couple of hours of reminiscing we stopped and realized that we weren't kids any more and that what we both had been feeling all these years was love. To say that I was happy would have been putting it mildly. I was ecstatic, reborn, and flying as high as the moon. My life had come full circle. We were together again. Just looking into her eyes and hearing her voice lifted my soul. Taking her home and leaving her at the door was the hardest part of our reunion. My feet wouldn't move, for fear that I'd never see her again. She must have sensed what I was feeling, because she came back to the door and said, "Joe this is just goodnight. I will see you tomorrow, right?"

"Tomorrow and every day of my life, angel. But, for tonight I'll see you in my dreams."

*C*hapter 9

"Joe I have always seen you in my dreams. Tonight's dream will finally be of us together at last."

God had answered my prayers after all. My sweet angel Rose was back in my life once more. Nothing would ever separate us again.

It took us a month to explain all the changes we had gone through. We talked about what happened to Rose's family and what had happened to mine. She listened to everything I told her about the years since we had been apart. There was no doubt or pity in her eyes, just love. Her life story wasn't a pleasant one either, but we'd both survived the hurt and loss we'd gone through, and were somehow together again. That next year was a walk in the clouds. We were only apart when we had to work. Her family welcomed me with open arms and my brothers loved her like a sister. What was not to love about her? She had grown into a loving, beautiful woman with a heart of gold. I was well into my surveying career with Mr. Ludlam, when I decided I couldn't live without my angel anymore.

We went to Christmas mass together and walked to the park afterwards. While we were sitting on the swings, it began to snow. I put my arm around her and wrapped my coat over her shoulders. Snowflakes fell softly on her cheeks and I kissed them away. "Rose, I can't give you all the beautiful things you deserve, but if you marry me, I promise to give you my heart, my soul, and a lifetime of happiness. And all the beautiful things, someday."

She cradled my face in her hands and said, "It's about time. What took you so long? I can't wait for us to be married."

We kissed a long passionate kiss and watched the snow falling on that night we would never forget.

As we started walking home, Rose told me something I'd never forgotten. She went back to the first time we had met. After taking the donuts I had just sold her, she ran right to her sisters and told them "I've just met the cutest, red-haired boy and someday I will marry him." Wow. I couldn't believe that she had the same feelings as me way back then.

Of course her sisters laughed at the precocious little girl back then, but she said, "They won't be laughing at me now."

After that enlightenment and her agreeing to marry me, I floated on air all the way home. How unbelievable could life be? Would anybody ever think that such a thing is possible? Could two young children foresee what the future had in store for them when it came to matters of the heart? Was there some kind of spiritual thing going on between us? Despite all the years apart, we had found our way back to each other.

Everything was coming together finally. The years in the orphanage had toughened me up and they taught me to look beyond the moment and, to go for the gold ring. In this case, the gold ring would be the one I put on Rose's finger. That would be our bond for life, no forever. I knew in my heart that mama would be happy for us. If only she could have met the woman of my dreams. "Someday mama" I thought to myself. I promise to make sure that you will always be a part of our life too. That was an extra prayer I had in my heart. Right then and there I felt as though I had a special connection with God and the angels. Maybe I did.

I guess the man up there can fix anything. We were together again. I whispered a silent prayer of thanks to God, and vowed to make a life of love and happiness for Rose and me. I lay awake for hours just seeing her face before me and hearing her soft voice in my head. I thought, *There is nothing on this earth that will ever keep us apart again. Goodnight, my sweet angel. I love you, Rose. Forever. I'll see you in my dreams.* And I did.

Sam was happy, too. He had just married a girl, Vinnie, whom he had met soon after coming home from the CCC camp. They had set up an apartment in Brooklyn for the two of them. Mike, Lou, and I still shared the same apartment and would miss seeing Sam but we were happy for him. It was time for us. We were men now and working good jobs. I told my brothers that I had popped the question to Rose, and we would be getting married too. After a couple of nights had passed, Mike told us that he had plans for himself also after Rose and I were married the next year. As soon as he turned eighteen, he was going to join the Navy. He always loved the sea and dreamed of riding the waves to foreign lands. I hated the thought of Mike being away from us, but he was a man now too, and he was entitled to live his dream. He promised to keep in touch and that nothing would ever change the fact that he loved his brothers and would always be a part of us.

Chapter 10

We had to get together and decide how we would be taking care of Lou. He was still too young to fend for himself and he wasn't very ambitious. In fact, we were all worried about the attitude he had picked up at the home. He had a devil-may-care way about him that often rubbed us the wrong way. Well, he would have to move in with either Sam and Vinnie, or with Rose and me. Sam talked to him, I talked to him, and Mike just threw in the towel. Lou had a year to make his choice and that was that.

One night on his way home from work, Sam saw Lou standing on the corner of his block talking to some unsavory guys. Sam knew these guys were connected, and couldn't understand why Lou was so far away from his home with Mike and me.

Sam called Lou over to him and told him that he was taking him to our apartment for a talk. Lou was reluctant, but Sam was the boss, so he followed. When Sam and Lou arrived at our apartment, Sam threw the door open and with one hand, flung Lou to the floor. Sam was red-hot pissed. Lou had bounced like a rubber ball, but the sneer on his face was like a knife in Sam's heart. Mike and I had no idea what was going on and tried to block Lou from Sam. My brother Sam took his papa role that had been thrust upon him seriously. There were times when he would not take lip from

28

any of us and didn't hesitate to land a swat or two to our body or what ever was closest to him. This looked like one of those times when Lou was going to be getting some of that built up rage that festered in Sam. Lou knew he was wrong in being out so late and so far from home, but when he asked Sam why he was so angry, he got a kick in the butt and an order to shut up.

Sam screamed at Lou "We are good and honorable Sicilians. We do not associate with Mafioso."

Lou tried to explain "But I don't know those guys, they were only asking for directions."

Sam shouted "Directions. You are so stupid to think I would believe that lie. I give you fair warning. If I ever see you with any of that scum I will be the one to break both your legs before they do."

We calmed him down and with a slap to Lou's head he left. Mike and I hoped that Lou had learned a lesson that night. Be a man to be proud of, and always keep your family close. But Lou fooled us all. Two days later he went missing. We searched everywhere for him. Day after day went by and we still had no idea where he'd gone. Nobody had seen or heard from him. Sam was worried sick that he might be with the wrong guys again. The three of us had started to think the worst.

Two weeks later we received a letter from Lou. The crazy kid had lied about his age and joined the Navy. In a way, it was kind of a relief to know that he was all right but Sam was disappointed in Lou. He thought the kid should have acted like a man and faced his brothers with what he had done.

I told Sam "He is just a kid after all. Maybe a stint in the Navy will make him grow into the man we would all be proud of."

At least he wasn't in trouble and we weren't at war. So I prayed "God speed little brother. Come home safe and matured."

All of a sudden four of us were going our separate ways and there was still no word on Angelo, Tony, and Phil. It was time now to broaden our search for our missing brothers. I knew in my heart that one day we would all be together again. It happened for me and Rose, and it would happen for our brothers.

Chapter 11

But for this time, my life would begin and end with Rose at my side. Sam was married, I was getting married, Lou was in the Navy, and Mike would be in the Navy the following year. Four brothers had become men now, and that was what life was all about. Living and loving.

I was having dinner with Rose's family one Sunday when she took me aside to tell me a secret. We went into the parlor, away from the others, and settled into the big soft sofa by the window. She told me that since her older sister Jenny had gotten married Gene had started talking about maybe marrying his girlfriend Inez. "That's good news, isn't it?" I said.

"Oh no Joe. Gene isn't ready for marriage yet. Mama would just die if he left home so soon."

I explained that Gene was three years older than me, and that if I was ready, then why shouldn't he be ready? Rose felt that because her father had died and even though her mother was remarried, Gene was still like a father to her and her brother and sisters. Besides her mama had another baby, Anna, and she was pregnant again.

It seemed the stepfather wasn't working out too well with all the kids and was threatening to leave. Even his own kids were hoping he would leave. "Then what would mama do?"

I told Rose, "Gene is the kind of man who would always be there for his family even if he was married. And are you forgetting that we will be married soon and your family will be my family too?"

This was the family I hadn't had for years and I was thrilled at their acceptance of me as a brother and son already. " I too will always be there for your mama."

Rose and Gene had always had a special bond and I could understand how she must have been feeling about his getting married. She told me stories of how he had protected her since she was a baby. He even had me checked out before we became a couple. Right from our first meeting he was like another brother to me. Gene was a tall, dark-haired man. He had the good looks, plus the kind and caring personality of his family. I could see from the first time I talked to him that he loved his little sister very much. His love for his mama and siblings had no bounds. He was a good man; he was gentle, but strong of heart. He was the friend I had never had when I was in the home.

Rose calmed down and said that Gene would have to get married before us, because he was older than Rose and that was the proper way to show respect for one another. I understood and knew what she was thinking. Our wedding would have to be postponed. That wasn't a set back that I was happy about, but Rose had a good point. Gene was the eldest and should have the respect of his little sister. I too respected Gene too much not to do the right thing for him and Inez. So I decided to talk to Gene about our decision.

What a guy. His first words were "Don't worry kid I won't mind waiting till after you two are married." I protested and told him that wasn't the reason why I wanted to talk to him. I wanted him to know that Rose and I had already decided to postpone our wedding.

He put his hands on my shoulders and said, "You two were destined to be together. Rose has been waiting for you long enough. I've watched her for years searching and yearning for the chance to be with you again. If you don't marry her when planned I'll be very disappointed. Besides I'm tired of her using the rouge I bought for Inez and had hidden away for

Christmas. She thinks I don't know about that, but she's so cute I could never be angry with her." At that moment and for the rest of my life, I loved Gene, and if possible, as much or maybe even more than my own brothers.

Gene and I told Rose of his decision, and she burst into tears. He held her in his arms and told her his wish had always been for her happiness. Besides that, he said that Inez had no idea of his intentions, and a wedding would be a good place to pop the question. So that was that. Our wedding plans went full steam ahead.

Rose and I decided to have our wedding ceremony in the church that had, through a miracle, brought us back together. The memories we had of Old St. Patrick's Church and the Chrystie St. Park would always be a part of our love story. Rose's birthday was in February and mine was in March so we planned the wedding for June 28, 1936. Rose would be seventeen and I would be eighteen. We were ready to conquer the world, or at least our little part of it. Rose's mom and her brothers, and sisters were so happy for us.

The whole family pitched right in helping us with our plans and needs for the big day. We were able to find an apartment in the same building where Sam and Vinnie lived. The apartment was in a six-story building, on a nice, tree-lined street on Meserole Street in Brooklyn. The area had a mix of Jews and Italians, just like Little Italy. It was a trolley car ride away from Prospect Park, for a nice country-type outing, and Knickerbocker Avenue, for a great selection of shopping. We would be near the Williamsburg Bridge, and at least two, big Movie theaters. It was Perfect. Everything was moving along at a steady pace and it was just perfect.

Chapter 12

And then pow! It hit the fan and the walls came tumbling down. Life has a way of hitting you in the gut, and always at the wrong time. Here we were all keyed up as the wedding was getting closer every day, when mama Anna was thrown for a loop. Her marriage was over. The old man left, and mama was looking for a new place to live. Fortunately, she found a really nice place in Ridgewood. As beautiful and strong as my future mother-in-law was, she picked up her kids and moved right away. By that time she had another baby girl, Florence, and the step-kids, who were older than mama's kids decided to be on their own. Of course, they would always be a part of mama's life, as she had grown to love them too. Mama was fearless. She assured all of us that she was happy with the change, and she would have no problems raising her children. After all, her eldest daughter, Jenny, was married to Rocco, had a nice apartment in Manhattan, and was pregnant. Her second daughter, Rose, would be married to me soon, so her future was secured. Mama knew that her eldest son Gene was courting Inez and was sure to be married soon too.

So Mary, Paul, Lena, Anna, and Flo would be at home with mama. Somewhere in the not too far future, all of her children would be off on their own but until then, they were her immediate future. And she couldn't ask for anything more to fulfill her life. What a woman. Mama Anna was the hardy beauty of Palermo, Italy. Our families had never met but their customs and lifestyles were exactly the same. She had blonde hair and blue eyes that were passed onto her by her mother, as my mother's family had passed on to her, the red hair and hazel eyes.

They were both peasant girls who had fallen in love with men from their homeland. Mama Anna met and fell in love with Bartolomeo, a tall, fair-skinned man with blue eyes and a glorious mane of black hair. They both decided to strike out for America as soon as they were married. Their adventure to a new world both saddened them, and yet gave them joy. Only one sister, Anna's, followed them to New York. The rest of their families became only a memory, since they were never to see them again. Their love for each other blossomed and grew deeper with each new year in America. Her lover's sudden death after twenty years of marriage almost killed Anna. But for her children and the baby growing inside her, she might have just faded away. She kept them in her arms and close to her heart and they kept her alive.

Every Sunday was family dinner time at mama's, after mass, of course. What a gathering. Mama and the girls made lasagna, meatballs, bracciole, lentil soup, and salads. Mama loved to bake and made cookies better than any bakery. It was guaranteed that those cookies would make their way to our wedding table. She worked miracles with the big, black, iron, coal stove. When the iceman came, he filled the icebox with a big block of ice and mama filled it with delectable leftovers.

No matter how much she cooked and for so many, there were always leftovers. Mama's sister and brother-in-law had opened a small, family style grocery nearby and planned to supply the food for our wedding. Mama was making Rose's wedding gown, she was also a fine seamstress, and the church gave us permission to use their gathering room for our reception. Everything was once more moving along smoothly.

Chapter 13

Our apartment was almost ready, and Rose and I were looking for furniture. All I wanted was a comfortable bed and a cozy, mohair sofa. We were busy measuring the rooms one day when Sam came rushing in. He was all flushed and looked like he was ready to pass out. He grabbed my shoulders and started to cry. I had never seen him act like that before. It scared the hell out of me. "Sam, please what's wrong?" Rose ran to get him a glass of water, and I gave him my handkerchief. What Sam finally told us was beyond belief.

He cried out "Joey, Joey I found mama." At that we were both crying.

"How? Where?" I asked.

Sam said that he was doing a small electrical the job at the Bellevue Hospital when he struck up a conversation with one of the doctors. He briefly explained to the doctor the circumstances of our mama's hospitalization nine years prior. When he was finished the doctor told Sam that he would try to get to the bottom of what happened to mama and find out where she might be. Sam thought that was the end of that, but on that day he saw the doctor and he gave Sam the information he had gathered from fellow doctors. Mama had been transferred from Bellevue Hospital to the Pilgrim Psychiatric Center on Long Island. Her lack of English and her erratic behavior indicated that she had a mental and not a physical condition. So there it was. At last, we found mama.

So we knew where she was but there was still the question of, why she was there? "She's not crazy, Joey. She was sick physically not mentally, right?"

I tried to calm Sam as best I could but questions and memories were stampeding in my head too.

Could we find this hospital and finally get to see mama? After a while, we calmed down and started making plans. Sam would try to get more information from his doctor friend and I would ask Mr. Ludlam, my boss, if he knew where the hospital was and how to get there. What a conglomeration of emotions we were going through. We experienced love, sympathy, happiness, and great expectations. I thought, "Mama we will find you." It might seem futile to some but to us, nothing could stand in the way of being with mama again.

Time passed too quickly and still we knew very little. Apparently there were forms to be filled out proving our relationship to mama, and so we could get permission to visit her. We soon had the address and directions to the hospital but no way to get there. We needed a car and none of us knew how to drive one. Gene came to the rescue. He bought an old Model-T Ford and was learning how to drive it. One month before Rose and I were to be married, we received permission to visit mama. Gene, Inez, Rose, Me, Sam, Vinnie, and Mike squeezed into the car and headed for Long Island. Somehow, three hours later, we found the hospital.

Chapter 14

The hospital was big and overshadowed with gloom and doom. Inside, although clean and sanitary, it emitted an air of coldness and despair. The floor nurse led us into a parlor-like room and while the women sat and chatted, we guys paced the floor anxiously. The tension in the room was palpable. It seemed like an hour before the door opened and the nurse led mama into the room.

Sam, Mike, and I walked slowly towards mama with tears running down our cheeks and an ache in our hearts. She seemed smaller than we remembered as kids. She was about five feet tall and slightly built and she was still beautiful. Her long, red hair had turned white, and was rolled into a bun at the back of her head. Her big, hazel eyes were turned down and her head was bowed to us. She didn't seem to know where she was or who we were. Maybe she forgot us, or only remembered the small sons she had left behind. Or could it be that she really was mentally disturbed?

Sam took her hand and started talking to her in Italian. "Mama, bellisima mama. We are three of your seven sons, who have spent our lives dreaming of you and have finally found you." She listened to his every word without a show of emotion. Sam was starting to feel all talked out when mama suddenly gripped his hand and said, "Cara mia figlio." The barrier was opened, and we ran to her side filled with love and gratitude. Mama was with us again. Her eyes flitted from one son to the other. It seemed she couldn't get enough of how we'd grown and were with her again. She touched us, caressed us, and wouldn't let go of us. Mama wanted to know where her other four sons were. We didn't have the heart to tell her that we'd lost contact with Angelo, Tony, and Phil and we didn't think she would understand that Lou was on a Naval ship somewhere. Maybe later, but that was not the time. We just wanted to revel in our newfound joy at being with mama. We sat her down and introduced her to our wives and our new brother, Gene. We told her that we would come again to bring her home with us. She was smiling and vibrant and so happy. She said that she wanted to go home now and see her sons and papa. We were mortified.

How were we going to explain to her that she couldn't come home yet, and that there were papers to fill out and preparations to be made? We changed the subject and started telling her of our many accomplishments. Her whole demeanor abruptly changed. Her eyes grew dim, her body posture was listless, and she seemed to have frozen on the spot. We tried everything we could to get her back to us. We had no idea what had come over her so suddenly. Somehow, she had left us again. The nurse heard our panicky calls to mama and came running in. She went immediately to mama, checked her pulse, and looked into her eyes. We all rushed the nurse and demanded to know what was going on. She explained that mama had a sleeping sickness, and that we would have to make an appointment to speak with her doctor for a more detailed explanation of her illness. The nurse said that she could not divulge a patient's problems or treatment, and that only a doctor could do that. Sam went bananas. He demanded to see mama's records right away. But like everything else, there was a ream of red tape waiting for us. We could not get an appointment to speak with the doctor for two months.

Rose and I would have our wedding as planned, and Gene would take us all back to the hospital in August. Kisses and hugs were lavished on our unresponsive mama. It broke our hearts to see her being taken away in a wheelchair. I thought, "Just two more months mama. We will fight the world if necessary to get you home again." It just wasn't right. It wasn't fair to mama. Everything had been taken away from her, her youth, her husband, and her children. All she had left were faded memories, and a life that was nothing more than a subsistence. If only she had the memories that we had of her, and the happy times we shared before she had become so ill. There were good times.

She used to tell us stories of her life in Palermo, of the love her family shared, and how she had made a mistake in expecting more for herself. If her older sister Jeanette had not decided to leave Italy, she would still be there. She told us how she met our father on the boat to America, and how he shared his dream of a fruitful life in the United States of America with her. He was so kind and caring of her on the trip that she couldn't help but fall in love with him. When they arrived at Ellis Island, he helped with her few packages and with the questioning process. Two months later, she and papa were married and her sister moved to Connecticut. She didn't hear from her sister for two years. By that time mama had her first son, Sam, and her sister had married a fairly well-to-do older man. In mama's eyes her sister had deserted her and left her to the whims of an uncaring man (her sister was out of contact with her for forty years). By the time six of her sons were born, mama had become very despondent and although she brightened up when telling us her stories, she often lapsed into solitude afterwards. But she was with us again, and we would make the rest of her life one of love and happiness.

Chapter 15

One day, in the very near future, we hoped we would be a whole family once more. If only mama could have come to my wedding.

Rose and I welcomed June with the wedding of a lifetime. My dear, sweet, beautiful Rose was the most gorgeous bride anyone had ever seen. If ever there was an angel on earth, she was it. She was a vision of beauty in her long, white gown. Her blonde hair and her pink cheeks glowed from the light filtering through the stained glass windows of the church. The only thing missing from this spectacular sight were the wings she had worn the first time my eyes beheld her angelic beauty.

But she didn't need wings. She was my angel and I was floating on air. Every step she slowly took coming down the aisle made my heart flutter and skip a beat. Tears welled up in my eyes and my hands trembled. This day was the true beginning of our lives together forever. In just a few minutes, she would be my wife. The sacrament of marriage seemed to fly by, and all I could see before me was Rose. All I could hear was her "I do." We were suddenly kissing for the first time as husband and wife, and we were ready to run right out into our future. Love was in the air and all around us at the reception with our family and friends. There was singing and dancing and a lot of food. By that evening, we were exhausted as we headed out on our honeymoon. The only thing shared about our honeymoon was that it was everything we had ever dreamed of. Some things have to be kept personal you know. We were happy and sharing a love that would last through all of eternity.

On our way home to our new apartment, we talked about having to go back to work and being apart for nine hours a day. Rose insisted on keeping her job, so that we could put even more money aside for a home in the suburbs some day. I told her I didn't want her to feel that she had to work. I had a great job and could handle expenses and still save money. But she said she would feel bored at home without me there, and besides that she and Gene's, girlfriend, Inez, had become close since they'd been working at the same place. The hat factory they worked in produced all kinds of hats. It produced men's, women's, and children's hats in all sizes, styles, and materials. Actually, Inez was a little afraid of working there because of a frightening experience she had while busy at work. I loved Inez like a sister but I found her tale a little hard to believe.

Large tubs of material stood beside each worker as they made the hats. While bending over to pick up some material, Inez claimed that a mouse jumped up and as she screamed, it popped into her mouth. Of course she was able to spit it right out but she was terrified it could happen again. All this was supposed to have happened while we were on our honeymoon, so who really knows?

Apparently, that wasn't the only thing that happened while we were away. Gene and Inez came up to our apartment for a visit the first night we were home. Shock hit both of us as they walked in, and Inez had suddenly looked very pregnant. Obviously, Gene had fooled us completely. When he told us to go ahead with our wedding plans he and Inez were already married.

They had both decided to keep it secret because her mother was against their getting married, so they were married at City Hall, and the only one they told was mama Anna. Boy could they all keep a secret. I thought Inez had put on a little weight a couple of months before our wedding, but with the loose dresses she was always wearing I figured it was just the

44

clothes. Son of a gun. They told the whole family while we were away, and wanted to be the first to tell Rose and me. While we were setting up our apartment, they were doing the same thing for themselves. We were thrilled for them.

Now, Gene and I had something else to share. We were both married men and loving every minute of it. Ah, married life. Rose was everything a man could ever hope for in a wife. She cooked (great meals), she cleaned (you could eat off the floors), and she always looked like a goddess. I couldn't believe I deserved such love and devotion. She meant everything to me; she was my life, and my love. There was nothing I wouldn't do for her. Just thinking of her and the two of us together forever, sent shivers up and down my spine, the two of us together forever. Every hour of every day my heart rejoiced in our love.

Chapter 16

August came in like a blast out of hell. The heat was constricting and almost unbearable. We spent as much time as possible during the weekends at Coney Island or in the shade of Prospect Park. Rose had not been feeling well since July, and I was worried sick. She wouldn't go to a doctor and said that she would get over it soon. Well she didn't get over it. So we went to the doctor together. They had me sitting in the waiting room. I was holding back from breaking open the door to see how she was doing. Finally, the nurse asked me to come in, the doctor wanted to see me. Oh my God. What did he find? I thought to myself, "My angel, oh please don't be sick."

The doctor turned out to be Doctor Dora. She was a diminutive little woman with the biggest and brightest smile imaginable. I thought to myself "Don't smile at me and then give me bad news." When she started to speak, Rose held my hand and I broke into a sweat. She said that Rose was pregnant. The doctor said Rose was just experiencing morning sickness and that it would pass in a month or two. She also said I was not to worry about Rose doing her normal activities which included her job. Rose had wanted me to hear this from the doctor, so that I wouldn't worry about her like I always did. I just sat there speechless with a goofy smile on my face. Finally, I came to, and asked the doctor about Rose's health and how, when, and where was all this to happen. Doctor Dora

49

said Rose was a strong, young woman and she foresaw no problems. The baby, he or she, is scheduled to arrive by the end of April. Doctor Dora would be the attending physician and the "how" was between Rose and me.

Well, ok, I was glad to know that all was well but I couldn't help feeling slightly left out of the game. After all, we had just gotten married and had just started our journey of "us" forever. A baby might take all of Rose's attention. Was I being selfish? Could that really happen? Besides, how could we afford a baby? What happens to all the plans we made? This was all happening too soon. What if? What if? Just think, three of us forever? On the way home, Rose had read my thoughts. She was asking herself the same questions. She had wanted me to hear out the doctor so that I could be a part of this life experience with her. Wow, does anything get past this beauty beside me? Talking like this put a whole new prospective on the changes our lives would be facing from then on. We would embellish our love for each other with the love for our child. We would now be a family unto ourselves. Thank you Rose for making me whole.

Well, the doctor was right. Within a couple of weeks, the morning sickness had started to ease up and Rose was starting to get the glow of pregnancy. Otherwise, she really didn't look pregnant. She hadn't put on any extra weight and her tummy was as flat as ever. She was getting cravings though. She wanted caramel candy, of all things. That was fine with me. Anything she craved, I'd run for it. One of her symptoms of pregnancy was feeling tired at night. I asked her to give up her job, but she wanted to work for a few more months at least. By the end of October, after a couple of cancelled appointments, we were finally scheduled to see mama's doctor. I asked Rose if she would rather stay at her mother's house on that day instead of making such a long trip. She said she would like to spend the day with her family and hoped I didn't mind her not coming with me. It was just as well that she didn't come. We were ready to do battle with the doctor anyway.

Chapter 17

Inez and Gene had a beautiful baby girl they named Doris two weeks before our scheduled appointment. Sam told Gene that he would get a friend to drive us out to Pilgrim State, but Gene insisted he come with us. So Rose, Inez, and the baby went to mama Anna's for that day and Vinnie decided to stay home too. Off we went without our women. Me, Sam, Mike, and Gene. Gene was the only mild-mannered one among us. Thank God for that because we three brothers were all hotheads when it came to the horrors our family had endured. Gene would have his hands full this day. We were all anxious to get mama home. The day better have a good ending or we'd all be climbing the walls.

When we finally arrived at the hospital, we were led into the same room we'd been in the first time we had come to see mama. After twenty minutes or so, the same nurse we'd seen the last time came into the room alone. She said mama was in one of her sleeping modes and we could see her after our talk with the doctor. After another waiting period the doctor finally came into the room carrying an armload of papers. He was a short gray-haired man wearing horn-rimmed glasses and a white jacket. When he introduced himself his voice seemed to be coming from someone else. He had a strong bear-like voice that just didn't match his outward appearance. He was very courteous and said that he would like to go over our mother's informational history with us. What he told us and from what we had seen for ourselves, Mama would not be coming home today or ever again. We weren't the only ones who had lost so much of their lives; mama was living in hell for the past nineteen years. We could have never imagined how bad her life had become for her.

When mama left her family in Italy, she felt alone and frightened. She married the man she thought could take away her fears and make her happy. He was her greatest mistake. He was only around long enough to get her pregnant every year. He showed her no comfort or understanding, and left the raising of their sons solely to her. When she lost three of her babies, all girls, to the flu, he told her it was God's way of telling her she was no good.

Three times mama had been hospitalized and diagnosed with the flu. Her sons were good boys, but she always felt too weak to cradle them the way she wanted to. She never learned to speak English. It was not because she didn't want to, but because her brain couldn't grasp too much at one time. Her sons tried to teach this new language to her, but her head was always hurting her. Then when she was brought to this hospital, she knew her life was over. Her babies had been taken away from her; they were literally pulled from her arms and her husband turned away from her. When he said that, we all burst forth as one voice. "We always wanted to find mama but there was never an opening for us until recently." He calmed us down and said he understood our helplessness, but now we had an opportunity to see that we were never at fault. Yeah, tell that to a little kid whose whole life and family was suddenly taken away from him.

"What happened to your mother was a tragedy and a misdiagnosis." He went on to explain her illness in detail. In 1918, she was hospitalized with influenza. After leaving the hospital, she continually complained of weakness, headaches, and trouble with her eyes. About two years later, she developed tremors of her arms and legs, which grew progressively worse. She was admitted to the Bellevue Hospital in 1924.

52

Then in 1927, they transferred her to Pilgrim State. Her mental condition was considered to be potentially dangerous to her and others because she was depressed and delusional. We all vehemently disagreed with that statement. The doctor said this was where the misdiagnosis came in. Upon her arrival there, she was given a series of physical and mental tests. Daily observations found her attitude, gait, staring immobile expression, and muscular rigidity in both arms to be the typical Parkinsonian syndrome. But in January of 1932, it was finally found that her true diagnosis was epidemic encephalitis. This was the disease that had started in her sometime in 1918. What therefore is encephalitis and what are we doing for your mother? First of all, it was commonly called the sleeping sickness. Symptoms began with fever, headaches, and joint pain. If left untreated the disease goes into its second stage causing confusion, reduced coordination, fatigue, and sleep disorders. All of these symptoms can be very deceiving and usually lead to misdiagnoses. How she caught it, when, and, where are questions that could never be answered after all these years. Although this was basically a mental institution, this was where she had to remain. She was transferred to this hospital, which was fortunate because we had this particular building that had a special area for patients with similar disorders. When he was finished and we had read all of the papers he had brought with him, a stunned silence fell over us. We were all in a state of shock and totally distraught over the thought of mama never coming home again.

Poor dear mama. She was sick for so long and did her best to care for and show her love for her seven sons. It wasn't her fault and it wasn't ours. It just wasn't fair. If only her illness had started when we were older. Maybe we, could have helped find the truth.

I couldn't hold back anymore and I said "This means we can't take her home and care for her?"

"No" Sam cried. "There must be something we can do for mama."

The doctor explained that she needed around-the-clock attention. Her sleeping came on at different times, and could last for days at a time, therefore she needed to be fed and medicated intravenously. There were also times when her neurological functions left her disoriented and unfamiliar with her surroundings.

"Isn't there a cure for this?" Sam questioned.

The doctor's reply dashed all hopes. He said that once the disease reaches its second stage, which it had for mama, there was no cure.

"Can she die from this disease?" Mike gasped.

In a hushed tone, the doctor said, "Damage caused in the neurological stage leads to mental deterioration, possible coma, and death."

Sam voiced our thoughts. "So then she will only get worse? Will she suffer?"

"The hospital has the means to keep her as pain free and content as possible. I guarantee that she is in good hands," the doctor told us.

For the past five years, aside from the encephalitis, she was physically, in good health. Her heart, lungs, and all of her vital organs were working perfectly. Death for her was not imminent. She could possibly outlive her doctor who was already seventy, though he didn't look it.

Through all of that I had a burning question. "Since our mother does not speak English, how did she tell you the things she did?"

"She didn't," he said. "A surprise visitor did."

We all looked at each other in astonishment and asked, "Our father?"

"No, I'm sorry to say, but let me explain." This was the day to change our lives in many ways.

Chapter 18

What he began to tell us shocked us to our depths. Since 1932 the hospital had been trying to locate mama's family. By 1933, they had still not found papa's whereabouts, and the orphanage we were in had no records of where we had gone after leaving there.

It was as though mama's whole family had dropped off the earth. Further probing led them to at least one child who had been adopted. "Angelo!" we all cried out as one.

"Yes," he said. "Now you ask, how do I know that? The adoption information was unwillingly given to Pilgrim State and we found the people who adopted your brother."

His tale became weirder and more interesting by the minute. We were all ears. Angelo's adoptive parents requested a meeting with the doctors to add any further information they might have had. This was a Godsend. The hospital needed any and all the information they could gather about mama. His adopted parents names were Frank and Connie. Because Angelo was too young, they came to the hospital without him. The new parents explained that Angelo had always known that he was adopted and he still remembered his family. Because of his unforgotten ties to his family, he was never officially adopted. That decision would be his choice when he got older. These two loving and caring people were also from Italy, but had moved away from Little Italy in 1926. They had a small house for the three of them in Corona, Queens. Connie was Sicilian and Frank was Neapolitan, so between the two of them they could speak at least four Italian dialects. This was great news for the hospital staff because they had not yet been able to communicate verbally with mama. Frank and Connie said it would be an honor to meet with mama.

They spent the next several hours of that day, and on the following day another few hours with mama's doctor, and conversing with mama. The new doctor they met with told them in graphic terms of the illness that their son's mother had and what they were doing for her. He also told them about the remaining six brothers who lived at the orphanage.

He told them that the six brothers whereabouts were unknown since leaving the orphanage in 1932. When he asked about Angelo, and if he had any knowledge of his background Connie told the doctor that Angelo was the son they had always dreamed of having and that they had told him very little about where they were going this particular weekend. When Frank and Connie were introduced to mama, who had no idea who they were, an immediate friendship was struck between them. By the second day, mama's life began to unfold before them. She told them of her life in Palermo with her mother and siblings. Her journey to America with her sister had been both exciting and terrifying. When she married her newfound friend, he changed her life. She loved her sons and was full of sorrow over the loss of her three infant daughters. When she grew ill, no one understood what she was feeling. They didn't speak Italian and when they spoke to her husband, he said that she was just a complainer. If they had only spoken with her sons, she wouldn't have lost them and been left to die with strangers. Her sons were old enough to tell them what she couldn't.

When Frank and Connie tried to explain their relationship with her son Angelo, she went silent. They tried to tell her that Angelo was well and wanted to be with her, but their words fell upon deaf ears. They promised to find all of her sons for her, but she had slipped into her sleep of forgetfulness. During the next four years, Frank, Connie, and Angelo visited mama every

Christmas. Though they tried, they still were unable to locate the rest of us boys, our father, or our aunt. On most of their visits, mama was unresponsive to them. Angelo had grown to love his mother more and more with each visit. He vowed to find his brothers once he was finished with school.

Hearing all of this made us feel good to know that we brothers were all of the same mind. Someday we would be together again, I swore.

We didn't have to be hit over the head with a brick to know that our fight to bring mama home was futile. She would live out her life in this institution. We never did get to see her on this visit because she slept through the whole day. We vowed to visit her often and try to get her to know us as grown men. The doctor agreed to keep us well informed of her health and if there was anything that we could do for her. At that point it was definitely time to do everything in our power to find our brothers. The doctor said he would contact Angelo and his parents to make plans for a reunion. He would also call the nunnery in the Bronx for information on the two of our youngest brothers. We couldn't ask for a better doctor for our mama than this one before us. Having him at our backs was just the thing we needed to push us on in our fight to put all the connecting pieces of our family together again. We needed to be connected again, and we would be.

On the last visit, the nurse took us to mama's room. She was sound asleep and we couldn't stay any longer. We sat at her bedside for a little while, and as we readied ourselves to leave, we all stepped around her bed and kissed her cheeks. Her face was calm and blissful as if she was in a happy place in her dreams. As we leaned over her to say goodbye a little smile curled around her lips and we heard her whisper, "Figlio Mio." Something deep within her told her that her *figlios* (sons) were at her side. Well that was the truth. We would always be at her side and she would always be in our hearts.

Chapter 19

On our way back to our homes, we started making plans again. The first thing we did was meet with Angelo. We had his address and decided to visit him on our way home. Corona was a beautiful little town in Queens. We found his home on a tree-lined street filled with clean, little houses that we'd only seen in the movies. It was like a scene right out of "It's A Wonderful Life" with Jimmy Stewart. Before we got out of the car, a handsome young redheaded man was out his door and running towards us. It was Angelo. Between the hugs, kisses, and tears we all managed to introduce ourselves. I don't know how it was possible, but he remembered all of us except Gene, of course, whom he took to immediately. Gene stepped out of our embraces to speak to Frank and Connie who had also come out to greet us. After we were all herded into their home, we went on and on about our lives and Angelo's. There was sorrow mixed with joy as we spoke of our lives apart from each other.

Angelo was a great kid who was full of love and concern. It was so easy talking to him, as if it was nine years earlier and we were all still kids. Frank and Connie were everything we expected after our meeting with the doctor. They were the kind of parents we had always dreamed of. Angelo was lucky to have them, and we could see their love for him was true. From then on they were family to us too. We all decided the next visit to mama would be a united one. That Christmas would be a happy gathering of the clan. If we could only find Tony and Phil, the family would be complete. That was the second part of our plan.

Gene had some friends in the Bronx who were able to get the address of the home that Tony and Phil were sent to. The week after finding Angelo, we all went to The Sisters Of Charity Home For Infants. The home was set on a hill beside a church and several buildings. We went to the rectory and were directed to the building for infants.

The Mother Superior of the home greeted us and escorted us to her office. When we explained our reason for being there, she told us that the boys would no longer be there because they are no longer infants. After seven years, the state welfare had them transferred to one of the four orphanages in the state, and they had not been adopted up to that point in time. Well, that part was a little bit of good news anyway. Thank God they hadn't been adopted. We hoped.

As usual, there was still a problem. The Mother Superior had no idea which home they were sent to, and whether or not they were together. Oh boy, that didn't sound very promising. We had just hit another brick wall. The lovely woman that she was, she offered to do as much as possible to help us find our brothers. Any information she could gather she would send to us immediately. The best thing we could do, she recommended, was to get in touch with the state welfare people as soon as possible. She gave each of us a beautiful crystal Rosary, and said that she would arrange to have a novena for our brother's return to us. We couldn't thank her enough for all she had done for us and made sure to put some money in the poor box in the church. We headed for home with some hope and a little more information to follow up on.

Chapter 20

The weather was getting colder and colder. The days just flew by and suddenly it was December. We had been running into one dead end after another in our search for Tony and Phil. It was almost 1937, and ten years since the beginning of the end for my family. At least five of us were together and inseparable. Angelo had become a permanent part of our family, but we still yearned to have the little ones back in the fold.

Pop was long gone and we never really looked for him. He gave up on us and I guess we felt we were giving up on him too. But we couldn't complain. Happiness had come to all of us at last. Sam and I had happy marriages, Mike was getting ready to join the Navy, Lou loved his life in the Navy, and Angelo would be graduating from high school and getting his future set. We four brothers got together every weekend. We wanted to make up for lost time, and we sure did.

The anticipation of seeing mama in the following weeks was giving us all some drive. Sam soon got a car, so Gene could stay home with his wife and new baby when we went to Long Island. My work was getting slow now because of the weather, and the money was coming in slow too. It didn't matter about the money though when it came to Rose. She was starting to look pale and weak. I wanted her to quit her job, but her doctor said she just needed to rest more in the evenings and on the weekends. So Rose relied on her doctor's word and kept on working. I knew she was only working because my job was so slow. I decided to get a second job. Then, she couldn't refuse my wishes for her to stay home.

Chapter 21

When I was away in the CCC camps, I had seen a young kid playing with a pair of spoons. He was actually keeping to the beat of the music on the radio and it sounded pretty good. I asked him to show me how he did it and when he showed me, I had to try it myself. Before long, I was playing along with the top bands on the radio. One day I had an idea that brought something new to my life. Since we were working around lumber all day, I picked up a couple of hard pieces of wood, carved them into thin strips about five inches long, one inch wide, and then sanded and shellacked them.

I had created my own set of "bones." When I rapped them together, they sounded like tap steps from Fred Astaire and muted timpani. I had discovered a talent I never knew I had. I had rhythm and I could make music from two sticks of wood. I was pretty good, if I did say so myself. I entertained the guys in the camp, and before long, we were all creating music. Sitting around the campfire at night, lonely and tired, we all needed some fun.

While I was at it, I made a set of drumsticks too. Every guy used what ever they could find, and so we had our own little band. Sam played trombone through his lips, I pounded every pot or table with my new toys, guys used washboards, tin cans, water glasses, and just about anything they could make music with. Well, it was more like a cacophony of noise, but we had a lot of fun anyway. I was playing a variation of drums and clappers. We gave each other silly names like "Windy" for Sam, "Bathtub Harry," and so on. I was "Joe Bones" and that name stayed with me for the rest of my life.

So there I was years later looking for a second job when it hit me. Why not put my bones to work for me? On one of my days of no work, I went to a music studio in Manhattan. At first, they thought I was some kind of a nut case, but then they had me play backup to a band rehearsing in the studio. The bandleader liked my use of the bones. He recorded his rendition of "Sweet Georgia Brown" with me in the background as backup. They liked the sound, gave me a copy of the record, and paid me five dollars. I thought, "Well alright," maybe now was the time to start using my unusual talent. I raced back to Brooklyn and stopped in at a little club that Rose and I had gone to once.

Somehow I had brass enough to play the record for the clubs manager, and I played my clappers along with the record. He didn't seem to be too crazy about my style, but he told me to come around on the weekend. He wasn't about to pay me, but if I was any good I could keep the tips. That was good enough for me, but I just had to convince Rose. It was not such a good idea after all. Rose loved that I found something that I really enjoyed fooling around with, but what if it was just fooling around? I would be spending a lot of hours at the club with no guarantee of making money, and most of all, she didn't want to see me disappointed. I promised her that if I didn't make any money on my first night there that I would give up the whole idea. Maybe I was just too full of myself. She started to cry and said that she didn't want me to ever give up on anything.

She put her arms around me, and held me so close that I could feel her heart beating against mine. "Joe, I said a foolish thing. You have never fooled around with anything. You have made a life for yourself and now for me and our baby. That proves how outstanding you are. Your strive for achievement has never failed and it never will. Have faith in yourself. I do. I love you, Joe Bones and so will the world. Go for it."

What a woman. What a life. I must be the luckiest guy in the world. As I embraced this most wonderful woman I thought to myself, "There is so much more of life to look forward to, so just grab the ring and make it all come true."

My first night was a bomb. I was having second thoughts, when Gene said he and a couple of friends would be coming to the club the following night. A couple of friends. My whole, combined family was there. Gene had done it again. He always came through.

What a night it turned out to be. Of course, my family rooted me on, but strangers seemed awed by the sounds that my two pieces of wood were making. Thank you, Gene. The next day, Gene told me that my face was as red as my hair, but I looked confident and my music had toes jiggling under the tables. The money wasn't bad either. Within two weeks, Rose and I were able to put aside the start of a little nest egg.

Chapter 22

It was time to see mama. Lou was on leave for a couple of weeks, so we five brothers would be going to see mama together. All of the women would be at mama Anna's preparing a feast of fish before midnight, and meat and pasta for the meal we would be sharing after we came home from midnight mass. This was a tradition among all Catholics, especially Italians. The birth of Christ had an even greater meaning for me this year because Rose and I would be having our own blessed event in just a few months.

Well there we were, five brothers on our way to see mama all together for the first time in ten years. The ride was uneventful. Everybody seemed to be lost in the same thoughts. Will mama be well? Will she remember us? And most of all, will we be able to make her happy, at least for tonight? Lou was the most nervous of all. He was pretty young when mama was taken away and he wasn't sure if he would remember her, or worse yet, would she remember him? How could she? He was a man now. We calmed him down as best we could because we were a little nervous too. The last thing we wanted was to upset or overwhelm her. As soon as we arrived at the hospital entrance, it started to snow. Now we had something else to worry about. Snow could make for a treacherous ride home and Sam, being a new driver, might not be very good at the wheel. Well, we thought what will be, will be. This was mama's time right then and there.

We were led to a large sitting room all decorated with holly wreaths and a Christmas tree with a crèche under its spreading branches. And there right before us, was mama sitting in a rose-colored velvet chair. Her long hair was tied in a bun, and her face was all shiny and pink. She was wearing a pink housedress and soft, pink fuzzy, little slippers. She was smiling as we walked towards her, and we stopped in awe of the beautiful mama we knew and loved when we were babies. We had just taken a giant step backwards into a past we had yearned to be in again for more than ten years. We circled her chair and she spread her arms out to hug us. One by one we kneeled before her, as she hugged us and called out each of our names. Our tears were running down our cheeks as we kissed her. I still cannot understand how she could have known each of us after so many years and so many changes, but she did. We sat on the floor in a semicircle before our mama.

She looked from one of us to the next and then said that Sam, Me, and Mike looked healthy, but Lou and Angelo were too skinny. She scolded the two of them and said that just because she could not be with us, that did not mean that we could get away with not eating enough. The two kids promised mama that they would eat all their food from then on. We asked her how she was feeling and if she was content being in that place. How silly she said we were for asking such questions. The doctors took away her pain.

For two hours, we talked about the good years of our lives and how we were helping our little families to grow. We told her how much we loved and missed her. We never talked about the hurtful times in our lives.

We were there to make mama happy and that made us happy. Mama was always in our hearts. She was happy to hear that, but we could see that she was starting to get restless and looked ready to fall asleep. It was time to leave. We struggled with the realization that we would not be seeing her for a long time to come.

We hugged and kissed her and were about to leave when she said "Next time, you bring my babies to see me. Anthony and Philip should be here too. Now, go my loves and tell papa I'm safe here. He can't hurt me any more." We were so caught off guard that we were speechless. This was the mama we remembered. The doctors couldn't be right about her health. But why did she say that about papa? He may not have been the most loving of men, but we never saw him hurt her. The nurse came in for mama. As they were leaving, mama turned blew a kiss and winked at us.

There was complete silence in the car ride home. None of us understood what had happened to mama. She remembered all of us and spoke of her love for each of us. She even asked for Tony and Phil. And yet, something was not completely as it should have been. Why would she be content in being away from us, and why would she say such a cruel thing about papa? We knew that some way, some how we would get the entire truth about mama. There was no giving up on mama, ever. Our search for our brothers had to continue and wherever Aunt Jeanette was, we would have to find her too. There were too many unanswered questions. Another piece of the puzzle was papa. Where the hell did he disappear to, and should we include him in our search for the truth? I wasn't the only one thinking these thoughts. Just before we reached home, we all started babbling at once about the same things I had on my mind. We were after all, of one mind. United again.

Chapter 23

The new year came in with one snowstorm after another. We were all still young enough that fooling around in the snow was great fun. Who cared how much it snowed? We had a winter wonderland as a playground wherever we went. Work was pretty much at a standstill for all of us. Surveying was impossible, the roads were impassable, and I sure didn't want Rose taking the train to Orchard Street. Yeah, she was still working. Her willpower was indomitable. The only money we had coming in was the little I made at the club, and even that was slow due to the weather. Not too many people had much money those days anyway so they were staying home a lot. We stayed home a lot too, but that was ok by us. We were nice and cozy in our little love nest with the radio supplying our entertainment and relatives dropping in whenever they could get through the snow-covered streets. January skidded out and February stormed in. Rose was looking more and more beautiful every day. She hadn't gained much weight, but she finally looked pregnant. We were happy and content with each other and with life itself.

Once every other week we took a nice slow walk to the movies. We went to the Rivoli theater, which was only about ten blocks from our apartment. It was an invigorating walk and Rose loved it. By the time we got to the theater her cheeks and nose was bright red. I gazed at her in wonder. She just glowed.

On the way home from the movies, we would stop at this little donut-making shop that made the greatest jelly donuts. The shop had come up with a swell idea. They stuffed the warm donuts with ice cream. Boy, were they delicious. We had to eat them right then and there, otherwise we'd have jelly and ice cream all over us on our walk home. Ice cream in the winter? It sounds crazy but it sure tasted terrific. We were on top of the world and we were in love.

And then, March arrived. Rose and I were about to face the biggest challenge of our life together. If we could have only known ahead of time what lay before us perhaps we could prepare for anything. But, that is not what is in the cards for any of us. We took what came along and ran with it, or we fell flat on our faces.

Chapter 24

Rose's kid brother, Paul, had started working with me for Mr. Ludlam. Every morning he would come to the apartment and we'd leave for work together. The weather had been pretty good for a couple of weeks, so we were able to work outdoors. This morning, March 2, Paul was right on time and Rose went to get him a cup of coffee. When I went into the kitchen, I saw Rose all doubled over and crying. "Rose, Rose what's wrong?" I was shaking like a leaf.

She was white as a sheet and holding tight to her little belly. "It's the baby Joe. Something's wrong. I'm bleeding."

That's all I had to hear. I told Paul to flag a cab and after throwing a coat around Rose, I carried her down to the waiting cab. Paul went to call the family and Rose and I rushed to the hospital. The poor cabby was as scared as I was hearing Rose moaning and crying in the back seat. I didn't have time to feel sorry for him though. I screamed at him to get moving faster and to not stop for anything. We made it to the hospital in fifteen minutes. Those fifteen minutes were sheer terror for me and Rose. But that was just the beginning of the fear that was to come.

When we arrived, Doctor Dora was already there waiting for us. I forgot that I had Paul call her too. The doctor had two nurses lead Rose to a room down the hall and told me that she would get back to me as soon as she checked Rose's condition.

Sit? Wait? Was she kidding? I couldn't stay out there waiting for my Rose. I had to be with her.

I got up and started walking, no, running to the room Rose had gone into. A big bruiser of a nurse stopped me by almost colliding with me. She told me in no uncertain terms that either I sat respectfully in the waiting room, or she would have me thrown out of the hospital. I was just about to give her a piece of my mind when I saw the doctor was headed towards me. "Ok doctor can she come home now?" I asked like a little kid. As she walked me back to the waiting room, she explained that Rose had gone into early labor and there was a problem. My heart stopped beating, and I wanted to hold my hands over my ears, but I couldn't move. No, no this can't be happening to my Rose. I begged the doctor to keep her safe, nothing must happen to her. I hung on to every word the doctor said, but I didn't understand most of it. All I heard was that Rose's life and the baby's life was both in danger. Life, danger. No, this couldn't be happening.

If my sweet angel didn't make it, I would die without her. If the baby didn't make it, Rose would be devastated. We both would. The doctor explained that the placenta that nourished the baby and kept it alive was coming out before the baby. This was called placenta previa and it was potentially life threatening to both the baby and the mother. The doctor was going to do everything possible to save both of them, but I had a very grave decision to make. A nurse would be coming in with important papers for me to sign. I would have to be the one to decide which life I wanted saved, Rose's or our baby's. She also said that Rose knew what was happening and wanted her baby to live. "We have to have your decision because right now Rose is not competent enough, being in a minor state of delirium, to make any choices." The doctor rushed back to Rose.

How could I not choose to have my angel live? I loved her with my whole being. She was my life. What could I do? She would hate me for the rest of my life, but I couldn't have her taken away from me that way. I knew she wanted that baby more than anything else in the world. She had been cradling it in her tummy, and besides talking to it, I heard her singing to it. It, it. This was our baby. I loved our baby too. I wanted our baby to live. How could I bear making a choice? The doctor came back with the papers, not a nurse. She looked as sad as I had felt. I signed the papers and she ran back to Rose. "God, please forgive me. Help me to know that I made the right choice. But most of all, keep my wife and our baby alive. "

One hour later, there was still no word. Mama Anna and the whole family had come to the hospital. I explained what was happening, but not about the papers I had signed. I was afraid that they wouldn't understand why I had made the choice I did. Mama Anna had brought Father Palladino with her, and he asked if he could see Rose and pray with her. Doctor Dora allowed the father and me in to see Rose, but only for five minutes. Rose smiled when we walked in. She looked so pale and weak. I held her hand and she said "I would like Father Palladino to perform the last rites for me and the baby."

I cried out "No, not that."

But Rose held my hand and said "Please Joe."

I squeezed her hand and started praying with the priest. I could see she was trying to be strong despite the intense pain she was in. I kissed her and said I'd be right back as soon as our baby was ready to see her crazy old man. Rose smiled and said "I love you Joe, forever."

"For all eternity, Rose." I walked into the hall, leaned against the wall, and cried. The priest was allowed to stay in the room so that he could baptize the baby as soon as it was born. I spent the next hour crying and praying.

Doctor Dora came in looking as though she had just run a mile and a quarter. She told me that I could go into the room now. I didn't ask her anything. I was afraid of what her answer would be. When I walked into the room the first thing I saw was Rose in her bed crying. I ran to her and held her tight. I thought, "Thank you, God. Thank you." My Rose was alive. I told her how much I loved her, and that I would take care of her always. She said she didn't know where the baby was. The nurses had taken the baby away so quickly that she didn't even know if it was a girl or a boy. She hadn't heard the baby cry and she was worried that something might be wrong.

Chapter 25

I was holding her and trying to comfort her when the doctor came into the room. She was carrying a very small bundle and smiling. "Well," she said "It's about time you two meet your beautiful baby girl." Rose and I were both crying, as she laid our baby in Rose's outstretched arms. There she was all four pounds, eight ounces of her. She was covered with dark hair and didn't cry, she squeaked. Our baby was an immediate star, and we loved every tiny bit of her. We laughed and cried and covered our baby girl with kisses. Rose checked her fingers and toes and ran her fingers through the baby's thick mane of hair. Doctor Dora told us the floor nurse would be in soon to take down our baby's name. We looked at each other and started laughing again. We never did pick out a name for our baby. Rose said that she would like to name the baby after my mother, but she had another name she would like to add. I told her whatever she wanted was, ok with me. Then Rose told the doctor that she had become a part of our baby's life the minute she was born and that she would love to name her after the doctor. Doctor Dora was flattered but said that Dora was only a nickname, her name was really Doreen.

Rose looked at me and said "Oh Joe that's perfect. Doreen Grace. How do you like that?" I loved it and the doctor was as pleased as punch. So on March 2, 1937 Doreen Grace officially entered our world. Now I had two angels to love. Thank you once again God, and thank you too Doctor Dora.

Rose was born to motherhood. She nursed and clothed the baby, cradled her and held her ever so tenderly. It was as if she had done this all her life. Of course growing up with her baby sisters, Anna and Florence had helped. But there was something special in the way she took care of Doreen. I guess after almost losing our baby had affected her more than anything else. The funny thing to me was that she and the baby seemed to have a special bond, it was as if their life and death struggle had brought them even closer together than a normal birth would have. It sure opened my eyes. The thought of losing either one of them lingered in my heart. Would she have ever forgiven me for making the choice I'd made? There had never been any secrets between us, but this secret I would take to my grave.

Rose teased me about my being afraid of holding the baby. Yes, I was afraid I might drop her, or somehow hurt her with my big heavy hands. By the third day, I finally held my littlest angel. I couldn't believe how she had already started to fill out and was becoming so beautiful. Rose and I were concerned that the delivery might have had some physical affect on such a tiny baby. The doctor assured us that although she had arrived a lot earlier than expected she was a good weight, and there were no physical abnormalities. She was perfect. On the fourth day of Doreen's life, the doctor told us that she had gained two ounces and would be ready to go home the next day. She said we might not be getting much sleep because Doreen would be feeding often. She had a lot of growing to do.

Our baby's lungs and vocal chords were getting strong enough to start doing some hearty crying. That was all great news and as far as I was concerned, our little girl wouldn't have to cry very much because we were going to spoil her with love and affection. We were on our own and headed home the next day.

Gene and Inez picked us up at the hospital to take us home. We were almost home when Rose saw what was playing at the Rivoli theater. It was, *Snow White and the Seven Dwarfs.* Rose loved Disney movies. She was a little girl holding her baby doll. Rose even sounded like a little girl begging to go to the movies. I couldn't believe that after everything she'd been through that she wanted to see a movie; she said this with a baby in her arms. We all tried talking her out of it. She still had to be careful and take care of herself and the baby, and not to mention it was still pretty cold outside. Rose was adamant. She wouldn't take no for an answer. She would walk slowly and nurse the baby in the dark of the theater. What could I do? Her strength had been keeping me going and I knew it would protect our baby too. Gene and Inez couldn't come with us because they had left Doris with Inez' sister Aura, and had promised to be home early. That was fine with us. We could always catch a trolley car or a cab. So, into the movies we went. We were three kids on a lark.

I have to admit that I enjoyed the movie too, and our little doll slept the whole time. It was a little chilly when we started for home, but thankfully we were all bundled up pretty good. It must have snowed a little while we were in the theater because the streets had a little dusting of snow on them. Fortunately, the sidewalks weren't icy or slippery. About three blocks from our place, it started to snow. Rose loved it. She licked at the snow falling on her lips, and made sure nothing was falling on the baby. This day had turned out to be a memory we would never forget. It was silly, fun and a little exciting, but most of all, it was our first family outing. It was all good and worth every minute of it. It would be one of the many memories we would have and laugh about sixty years from then.

As soon as we got to the apartment, I rushed to the bedroom and started setting out Rose's nightgown and fluffed up the pillows. When I turned around, Rose was standing in the doorway with the baby in her arms laughing hysterically. I looked at her dumbfounded. What had I done wrong? In between her giggles, she told me that she was not an invalid and our baby's bedding came first. The baby. What a fool. I was already forgetting our baby's welfare. Rose placed our sleeping angel on the bed and put her arms around me. "Oh Joe, I love you so much. You're the best husband in the world and although fatherhood is new to you, I know that you will be the best father in the world." How did she do it? She always made me feel so good no matter what I did. We looked at each other and wondered where Doreen would be sleeping. She had come so soon that we hadn't prepared everything we needed for her yet including a bassinet. Rose looked around the room and walked over to the credenza and opened the bottom drawer. It was the biggest and deepest draw in the unit. It would do for now. What a woman.

She emptied the drawer, had me clean it up, and lined it with baby blankets that her sister Jenny had made for our baby. She added her soft bed jacket, and topped it all off with soft muslin cloth she'd been collecting for the baby. Her beautiful, little hands had created a crib for Doreen. Rose turned our love nest into a haven for our family.

That's what we were—a family. All the questions I had been mulling over for months since Rose had become pregnant were answered. We had created a foundation and built a future.

Chapter 26

March had come in like a lion, as they say, and went out like a lamb. April, May, and June were the happiest of times for the three of us. Doreen had grown into one of the most beautiful babies I'd ever seen. Rose was magnificent in her achievements as a mother. And I, well although I was content with my life, I still wanted more for my family. I was still working as a surveyor with my brother-in-law Paul, and playing Saturday nights at the club. That was a good year so far. Only one thing had yet to be accomplished, and that was finding Tony and Phil. It was as if they had just vanished into thin air. We could find nothing in the system. We went to see mama for Easter and brought along Doreen. When mama saw Doreen in Rose's arms, she thought we had brought Phil to her. She cradled our baby in her arms and sang a soft lullaby to her. We didn't have the heart to tell her it wasn't Phil. But she did it again. Out of nowhere she said, "This little girl is the future." This time we were definitely going to talk to the doctor before leaving.

We managed to catch the doctor on our way out. After we explained the things she had said during our visits, he chided us for thinking that she was in any way out of her head. He said that her delusional moments were not a lapse in memory or perception, but rather an escape from reality during depression. Mama had been in physical and emotional pain for so many years that her only defense was to hide within herself. When she was medicated for her pain, she was as normal as anyone, It was during the onset of pain that she turned into herself, and found a place more comfortable for her.

The pain she had been enduring did not dissipate over the years, but had become more intense. Time was against her but seeing her sons was helping her to hold back the ravages of her illness. If only we could have taken her home with us. We could be with her every day. But that just wasn't in the cards for her. So back we went to our families. Little did we know that doom was heading our way.

Europe was in the throes of chaos. Germany was changing because of a little madman named Hitler. We worried about the country of our ancestors in Italy, but felt safe and secure in the country we were born in, America. Mussolini, although not the greatest either, could never throw in with a nut like Hitler. Thank God that all I loved and lived for was in the good old U. S. of A. Nothing could touch us here. Even President Roosevelt sounded unconcerned that we might be brought into the European problem. After all, we dealt with Germany once before and succeeded. All I wanted was to keep Rose and Doreen happy and healthy. The year 1937 was coming close to its last days and all was well.

Chapter 27

One quiet evening after Rose had put Doreen down for the night, we started reminiscing about the past year when she reminded me of an incident we had shared during the summer. My brother-in-law Paul had a good year of work and the money was getting better all the time. We were surveying all over New York. Bridges, roads, subways, and apartment houses were being erected like crazy. And then, one not so funny thing had happened to the two of us while Paul and I were surveying the backyards of some small homes in Brooklyn. It was a pretty old neighborhood with small grassy areas behind old track houses. It was nothing out of the ordinary for us. Paul was holding the plumb bob, a small ball on a string, and I was looking through my scope. I started motioning to him to keep backing up, when he suddenly disappeared. For a moment, I thought he was just being cute until I heard him screaming for help. I dropped everything and started running as fast as I could towards the sound of his voice. I came to a skidding stop just in time, because there was a gaping, six-foot, round hole in my path. Paul had fallen into a cesspool. Thank God he was alive, but the sewerage appeared to be at least waist deep. As I was leaning over the hole and reaching for his arms the earth cracked under my weight and I wound up right alongside Paul deep in the same ----. Then we were both screaming for help.

Suddenly, we heard a voice above us. We looked up and saw a woman leaning over her fire escape. She told us to hang on, and that she was getting help for us. Paul was starting to get weak and told her he didn't think he could stand under the pressure of the sewerage too much longer. She disappeared into her home and a minute later came back with a roll of heavy rope in her arms. We watched her tie the rope around the bars of the fire escape and her body, as she tossed the rest of the rope down to us. I told her we were too heavy for her, but she told me to shut up and start climbing. This woman was a powerful speaking woman, but how strong could she be? She was heavy-set and had big, wide arms but that didn't say much for the weight she would have to pull. So I tied the rope under Paul's arms and as she pulled, I shoved. Damn if it didn't work. Paul was above ground and safe. The rope was then thrown down for me, and she and Paul pulled me up and out. She pulled the rope from its supports and threw it down into the hole. Paul looked at me and went hysterical laughing. I wanted to hug him, but our combined odor was too strong. The next thing we knew, this big, beautiful, black woman was washing us down with a garden hose. She told us to keep our eyes and mouths closed while she sprayed our filth-covered clothing. When all of the clinging waste had been washed off our clothes, she told us to come into the building's hallway. She went into her apartment and a few minutes later came out with four, big towels. Her next orders were for us to remove all of our clothes, leave them in the basket next to her door, wash our bare bodies, wrap ourselves in the towels, and then come into her apartment. She turned, went through her door, and we hurriedly followed her orders. When we were as clean as possible, we knocked on her door and she let us in. She told us to sit at her kitchen table which was laden with cookies, small plates, and lemonade. She said, "Eat," and carried our soiled clothes into her bathroom.

We could hear the water running in her bathroom as she sang a hymn. Her singing voice was surprisingly soft and spiritually lifting. Her gruffness was just a cover up. She was a

God loving, generous human being. She was a wonder to behold and to know. We could hear her washing our clothes with a scrub board. We tossed around different ways in which to show our gratitude to her. Soon, she was seated at the table with us. She told us that her name was Tess and that she was a widow with two grown, married sons. When we thanked her, she just shrugged it off as a blessing from God that she was home at the right time. Then she excused herself and went back to the bathroom. There had to be something we could do for this wonderful woman. We'd have to ask her when she came back to the kitchen. We sat around eating cookies and recalling everything that had happened earlier.

One hour later, Tess came back with our wet and smelly clothes. She said she was sorry that she couldn't do anymore to clean them and that we'd have to wear them home. We told her how grateful we were and asked if there was anything we could do for her. She said, "Just get home to your families and make sure you throw those clothes away before you step into your home." She practically shoved us out the door almost before we were fully dressed. We thanked her over and over again. She shook our hands and said, "Lord but you boys stink. If you really want to do something, just tell God in your prayers that old Tess was only doing his bidding. And watch your step from now on." What a Godsend Tess had been. She would be in our hearts forever.

When we got to the subway, we had the car all to ourselves. I couldn't blame the other passengers for giving us a wide berth and looks of disgust. We did smell about as bad as a pig sty. Come to think of it, I don't believe pigs even smelled as bad. Anyway, we had a quiet ride home because we couldn't even stand being too close to each other. When I reached our apartment, Rose came running to open the door as usual and stopped short. She stepped back and told me not to set one foot in the apartment. I tried to explain what had happened, but she ran into the kitchen and came back with some paper bags, a wet washcloth and a towel. Now I was getting orders from her too. She told me to strip, wipe myself up, and throw everything in the garbage. So, like a bad little boy, I did everything she said and when I finished she led me to the bathroom where she had a bubble bath waiting for me. A bubble bath? What was next, some of her perfume? I thought, " She better not even go there." She threw a bar of Lava soap into the tub and handed me a scrub brush. She left the room saying she'd see me in an hour. "An hour? I thought, the water would be like ice by then." Well, this was a side of my angel I'd never seen before.

Exactly one hour later, my skin raw and freezing, I walked into the kitchen. The table was set for dinner and the food was warming on the stove. I sat sheepishly in my seat and waited for Rose's scolding. She set my plate down and sat across the table from me. I started to pick at my food. Rose giggled and then broke down laughing. "Hey," I said "What's so funny?"

She got up from her chair and came to me. "Is it safe to kiss you now?" She sniffed around me a little and then planted a big one on my lips. "Now that's my Joe." she said and started laughing again. We were both laughing and through my tears, I took her step by step through the experiences Paul and I had that day. When we finally went to bed that night, Rose said that we had to do something for Tess. We threw ideas around and finally came up with a big basket of fruit and Italian cookies for the woman who saved my life and her brother's. Rose would make up the basket the next day, and we could also give her something for Christmas. That's my girl. God bless her. Considering how badly the day had started, and how disastrous it could have been, I'd say that Paul and I were two of the luckiest guys on earth that day. Especially me. I had not only been saved by an angel of mercy, but I was able to go home and be loved by my own God-given angels Rose and Doreen. Amen to that.

Chapter 28

Sam stopped by one night and said he still had no news of Tony or Phil or even Aunt Jeannette. So what else was new? We were still no where in our search. He told me that Mike had enlisted in the Navy, and would be leaving by the first week in November. His outlook for Christmas at home seemed pretty dim. None of us had heard from Lou, but were hoping he'd have liberty and be home for the holidays. Well, hopefully we would all be able to be with mama for Christmas, otherwise it would just be Me, Sam, and Angelo.

By December, Rose and I were happier than ever and as pleased as we could be over Doreen's progress. She was walking and saying a few words and had turned into one gorgeous little girl. Who was prejudiced? Not me. Everybody said the same things about our little girl. They couldn't all be prejudiced too just because they were her family. Doreen's hair color had changed to a dark shade of blonde with red highlights, and bouncy little Shirley Temple curls that sparkled in the sunshine. Just like me she loved music. We would turn on the radio and while I played my bones and Rose sang along with the songs, Doreen had her own version of dancing. We had our own little jam sessions. Thank God our neighbors never complained about the noise we made tap dancing and playing the music loud and clear. I could never be a Fred Astaire or Bo Jangles but I loved to tap.

We had befriended a couple of our neighbors in our building and they became lifelong friends. Our next door neighbors were Jimmy and Pat who were newlyweds. Down on the first floor, the other couple we hung out with were Angelo and Adele.

They were married a year before us and didn't have any children at that time. Between our family and our friends, there was never a dull moment. These were the good times.

Mike and Lou did make it home for Christmas, so we five brothers all went to see mama. We brought her a carload of gifts. Mama Anna had baked a basketful of Italian cookies. Rose and her sisters and brothers filled another basket with knit sweaters, hats, shawls, and cozy slippers. Angelo's parents sent boxes of socks and pretty dresses. We guys chipped in and bought mama a cameo pendant that hung from a gold necklace. When the nurses saw all the presents, they were flabbergasted. We told them it would be a great thing for mama if she could share her cookies and other gifts with her friends there.

Mama was in good spirits when we arrived. As soon as we put the necklace on her, she said it was the best present she had ever received, and that when she was a little girl she had one just like it. All in all it was a good visit. When mama grew tired we had to pull ourselves away. It was a torment leaving her there. God, how we missed her. Leaving the hospital was the lowest time of our lives. Being men we felt that we couldn't cry, but there was a lot of sniffling on the way home. Our days of Christmas had become a mixed bag of feelings. On the one hand, it was wonderful to be with mama, and on the other hand, it was heart breaking to leave her again and again. If not for our new families and the love we all shared for one another, I don't know how any of us would have been able to cope with such loss and deprivation.

Chapter 29

And there it was another year. It was 1938. What could be expected this year? Maybe we would finally find Tony and Phil? Time would tell. I still had a nice steady job and my part-time gig on weekends. That was good. Rose and Doreen were my greatest blessings. I thought, yes, this would be a very good year. I just knew it. February and March made the three of us a year older and our life together had grown stronger. There was nothing better than having a beautiful wife to adore, and a happy baby girl to lavish all of our love on. By May, it was hotter than ever so we and our friends started having "tar beach" parties on the roof of our apartment building. Rose's sister Jenny, her husband, and sons visited us one day to join us on our roof. She couldn't get over the blankets spread out on the floor of the roof, and the large pizza pans filled with water for the kids to play in. While we were lazing around in our beach chairs, Jenny told us of a country resort she'd heard of in New Jersey. It was called White Hall Manor. The resort had small cabins on the shore of the lake or rooms in the magnificent inn. The meals were fresh, home-cooked, and served three times a day in their dining room. Behind the inn was a huge swimming pool and tennis courts. Jenny and Rocco were going to get more information, exact location, and costs, and hoped to go there that summer. It sounded great to both

Rose and I, but we wanted to consider going there the next year. We wanted to wait till Doreen was a little older.

The rest of the year was terrific. Doreen was growing like a weed and getting smarter every day. Sam and Vinnie had a son, Bobby, in November. I never saw Sam as happy as he was the day his son was born. He handed out cigars and from that day on he was never without a cigar in his hand. Mike was on a ship in the Atlantic and Lou was on a ship in the Pacific. They were having the time of their lives as sailors. That was good. Angelo was working with Sam in the Electrical Union. Sam had helped the union get a foothold in New York, and was loving it. That was good, too. But the strife in Europe was still going on and Japan was getting antsy also. That wasn't good. President Roosevelt felt the U.S. had no business getting involved with any of them, so we sat back and tried to live with that. Christmas came around fast and during that year, only Sam, Angelo, and I visited mama. She had put on a fair amount of weight and seemed more tired than usual. And there we were. There were good times, and not so good times all rolled into one to close out another year. Maybe the next year would be a better one for mama. All we could do was pray and wait anxiously for our next visit with her.

Chapter 30

The new year, 1939, started out cold and snowy. We played in the snow, went to the movies on Tuesdays and Thursdays, and sat around the apartment listening to the radio.

The shows we enjoyed the most were Jack Benny, Amos and Andy, and The Inner Sanctum. On cold dreary nights, we liked listening to that spooky show with its creaking door opening, while we snuggled up in bed. The only thing that was bothering us about the radio and movie newsreels, were the ominous reports coming from Europe. It seemed the only country trying to keep Hitler from their doorstep was the United Kingdom. Hitler. Even his name sounded creepy. He was one ugly guy. For some reason he reminded me of what Napoleon must have looked like. Fat chance that little weasel of a man couldn't be stopped. Well, he wasn't our problem. At that time we were looking forward to a summer of fun.

That summer we had already planned for a vacation at White Hall Manor, and we were going to have a wonderful time. Rose was so happy that we were going to New Jersey and she started making lists of what we would need for the trip. Her lists were enormous. You'd think we were going to be moving there instead of just vacationing. But she was happy and that made me happy. We started counting off the days on the calendar and before we knew it, July was just around the corner.

We decided to take the trip by Greyhound Bus because our vacation group had turned into a New Jersey invasion. Jenny, Rocco, their sons Freddie and Rocco Jr., Rose, Doreen and I were not the only ones going to White Hall Manor. Gene, Inez, their daughter Doris and their new baby son Bart were also going with us. Not to be left out, we were also joined by Sam, Vinnie, and their son Bobby. This was going to be one great vacation. We were all taking the cabins by the lake, so we'd be close to each other and less prone to be annoying to other vacationers with our fun and games.

After all, we were all young with small children and looking for a family retreat. We could all stand our own happy noise, but who could tell what other people might think of the clamor.

The bus trip was long and monotonous, so to keep the little ones amused we sang songs and played games with them. We sang until they fell asleep for the rest of the ride. I hate to admit it, but some of us guys fell asleep too. Guys tend to do that sometimes, especially when you're being rocked by a big bus whose wheels are rumbling underneath you, and the landscape is flying past your window.

Chapter 31

When we arrived at the resort, we were all pleasantly surprised. It was all, and more, than advertised. The main house looked like an estate of the wealthy. It was huge. A columned porch went around the whole house and was adorned with small tables, wicker chairs, and chaises, and lots of flowers and plants. Two large doors opened into a large foyer with a staircase leading to the upper floors. A long, teak table was near the foot of the stairs and there were two open rooms at either side of the foyer.

There were overly, large fireplaces in both rooms. One room was a richly furnished library or sitting room and the other was the dining hall. The furnishings in the dining area were tables, chairs and credenzas made of fine, solid oak. Damask seat coverings and linens were everywhere. This room could have easily catered to at least one hundred people. The two lower rooms equally shared a number of glass-paned doors leading out to the porch. It was gorgeous, simply gorgeous. This was class with a capital C. Wow. We were given a brochure with the directions, amenities, and dining times. Lunch would be served at 1:00 pm, so we all headed to our cabins while two young men carried all of our luggage.

On our way to our cabins, we saw a quaint covered bridge. Gene and I ran through the bridge and found a beautiful, Olympic-sized pool at its end. We ran back to the others and were mesmerized by the scene before us. We saw a sparkling lake surrounded by a white-sand beach and magnificent trees and shrubs lay at the center of a summer wonderland. To either side of the entrance to the lake were rustic, tree-shaded log cabins, a picnic area with a great barbeque, picnic tables, umbrella-covered beach chairs and so much more.

This country vacation spot was something none of us could have imagined even in our wildest dreams. Sure we saw places like this in the movies, but this was for real. City kids, who before were just barely making it, were living like the hoity-toity citizens. It was incredible and simply amazing. For seven days we lounged, swam, played, ate homemade bread and had four square meals every day. Our little ones had the times of their lives and by 7:00 p.m. were so happily exhausted that they were asleep almost as soon as their little heads hit the pillows. We spent our evenings dancing and chatting around a campfire.

Chapter 32

The first night there, the other vacationers joined us and one man in particular became my lifelong friend. His name was John. He wasn't married but was accompanied by a beautiful, young woman. Over the years, she was to become one of the many, beautiful women John would introduce to our family. John was the first Englishman I had ever met, and he came from a very well-known family in the arts. His mother was a poetess and his father was an artist. He loved the Bohemian way of life and relished his freedom to explore all areas of life. He was a free spirit who, when he found a true friend, gave his all to that relationship. He dabbled in photography and was a highly talented landscape and portrait artist. He was always sketching someone or something.

John had Rose and Doreen sit for a sketch he was working on, and said that he would have to finish it when he went home. We exchanged addresses and phone numbers and I was afraid I'd never hear from him again. We really had nothing in common with each other except a genuine liking of one another. He was well bred and extremely intelligent. I wasn't. Besides he lived in Greenwich Village and I lived pretty far away from him in Brooklyn.

One month later, he invited Rose and me to his apartment in the Village. We were dumbfounded when we entered his flat, as he called it. He politely asked us to remove our shoes before we entered the most luxuriously furnished room we had ever seen. Our bare feet sank into the softest and purest white rug imaginable. It was called a studio apartment, which was just one very large room. The ceiling had glass, skylight windows and the walls were painted a bright red with black accents. The furniture was all Chinese with seating, food mats, and bedding on the floor. There were paintings standing against the counter that led to the kitchen, and in the center of the room was a covered painting. When we were seated on the soft cushions he unveiled the portrait he had made of Rose and Doreen. It was exquisite.

I never accepted the portrait from him, only the sketch. I explained to him that his artwork should be in an art gallery and not in my humble home. He protested over and over until I told him that not only should his exquisite work be shown to the world but the thought of my girls being admired by that same world sent shivers through my soul. He became a welcome addition to our entire family and whenever he came back to New York from one of his worldwide visits, we were the first ones he called.

John's tales of his many adventures were spellbinding. I remember telling him once that he had taught me so many things about his world and his compassion for life that he had broadened my outlook of the power of knowledge. His response was that our love of family was more uplifting to him than anything else in his life, and that I should never take it for granted.

Chapter 33

The rest of the year went along as happily as usual. Doreen and our niece and nephews were getting bigger and smarter every day and the stork was on it's way again. Sam's wife Vinnie was pregnant, and our neighbor's wives Pat and Adele were pregnant too. Rose was happy for them, but I could sense that something was bothering her. One night I finally asked her if she was thinking of having another baby. Tears welled up in her eyes and she turned away. I held her close and tried to kiss away her tears but that just seemed to make things worse. I told her that even though we hadn't gotten pregnant again, it was ok by me because I was so in love with our daughter that I didn't think I would ever be able to love another child any way. I guess that was the wrong thing to say because she cried even harder. She wiped her eyes and after kissing me, said that she knew how I really felt about our getting pregnant again. "Oh, Joe did you truly believe that I had no idea about the choice you made when I was having Doreen?" I felt my heart drop. I couldn't look her in the eye. This was my biggest fear and it was happening as I'd expected. I'm going to lose my angel. "I realized when the priest wanted to baptize the baby right away that even though you knew what my choice was, your love for me was stronger than the love you hadn't yet shared with our baby. I understand. It's ok."

"A mother's love for her child begins at the moment of conception. A father cannot even guess of the love he will have for his child until he can actually see and hold his baby. I know how you must have suffered making the decision you did. I admit I questioned that choice you made. But the love you showed our daughter on that day, and all these many days later cemented the love we have for each other forever."

"I can never doubt you, ever. The tears I shed tonight are not for me, but for you and our little girl. I don't want to deprive you of another child, and I feel sorrow for not giving Doreen a sister or a brother to love. But I'm afraid, Joe. I don't want to take a chance that this could happen again. I don't want either of us to be put in the position of having to make a choice like that ever again. I would love to give you more children, but I just can't go through that again. Can you forgive me and try to understand what I'm feeling?"

Forgive her? Forgive her? I was the one who made the choice. I was the guilty one and not her. How could I not understand her fears? I have the same fears. There I was feeling sorry for myself, and not having the courage to be honest with the woman I loved more than life itself. For two years we kept a heartbreaking secret between us. Only she had the strength to face it and bring it out into the open. Right then and there I swore that I would always be honest and forthcoming with her. I let her know that she shouldn't fear being forthcoming and honest with me. I told Rose that I was very content and extremely happy with our life staying as good as it was right then until the day I died. She and Doreen were my whole life and if that's what she wanted then so did I.

"Don't worry baby, you have given me everything I have ever wanted and so much more."

So was it then. I didn't want my sweet angel living in fear or anxiety.

If it meant keeping my angel alive, and not putting her through the agony of maybe losing a child, then so be it. We may not be fulfilling one of God's plans, but He will forgive us. In the mean time, we have each other and Doreen would be getting all the love without having to share us. I hope someday she will still love us no matter what.

Chapter 34

The end of the year came and went after seeing mama and still not having any news of our two baby brothers. It had been a good year after all, and we were looking forward to another vacation in New Jersey. It was also an eventful year. I had made a new friend while on vacation and when we went to the San Gennaro Feast last September, I had another surprise, and this time it was right out of the past. We ran into a friend I hadn't seen since I was nine years old. We used to call him "Hardhead Mike" for a reason. I'll explain shortly. He looked great and after a lot of hugging, he introduced his wife Kitty to us. They had a little house in Canarsie and no kids at that time. Mike was born in Sicily and still had a slight accent. We reminisced about the good times we had as kids sitting on the fire escape, and smoking a cigarette that Mike had copped from his father. We were good kids though and never got into trouble. But sometimes things change as we get older. I was scooped away and he was scooped up in Little Italy. I asked him how he could afford a house. We were saving like crazy but it was still a few years away for Rose and me. He laughed and said he was Sicilian, wasn't he? Enough said. No more questions asked, and no answers needed. I still loved the guy and Rose and Kitty hit it off great. We were visiting them one day, when Mike pointed to a scar on his head and proceeded to tell Rose how he got it.

Mike, Sam, and me were sitting on his fire escape one hot summer day when he started to sing and dance around. He was always happy and loved to sing and dance when and where ever he could. Well, on that particular day, his dancing turned a little too exuberant and right before our eyes, he fell off the fire escape. It happened so fast that all Sam and I could do was scream as we watched him start his fall down six stories. We ran into the house and down six flights as fast as we could. What we hadn't seen was Mike fall head first through the glass roof of an old outhouse, and into the toilet bowl. By the time we got down there, Mike was out of the bowl and lying on the ground. His head was all bloody and his parents were crying hysterically. We thought he was dead until he suddenly groaned and started to get up. Well, to make a long story short, he had escaped death thanks to all the clotheslines he hit, and to the twenty stitches the doctor gave him. From then on, he was known as hardhead Mike. Rose was mortified, not only about his fall, which was horrifying enough, but just the fact that what he had fallen into was unspeakable. Mike just laughed and touched his scar. Good old Mike; he was still a happy-go-lucky guy, and I was grateful to have my old friend back in my life again.

Chapter 35

Anyway, we were now well into 1940 and enjoying every minute of the new year. All was well and all were happy. There was only one problem; the years seemed to be going by a little too fast. I thought, "Slow down time we still have a lot of living to do." It seemed like Doreen was just growing too fast. She and her mommy were always busy running somewhere during the day, and the evenings were a cacophony of laughter and playtime for all of us. What a joy it was to hear our little, girl carrying on conversations with us in her little baby doll voice. Maybe Shirley Temple was the child star of the silver screen, but to us . . . she couldn't hold a candle to our little star. Doreen could sing, dance, and roll those big brown eyes better than any child we knew. Biased? Proud? You bet.

The funny thing though was that everybody felt the same way about our little girl. I guess we were all spoiling her, but it was because she had such a charismatic way about her. Maybe it was just that she was so happy all the time. Rose's kid sisters took such a liking to her, that wherever they went and whatever they did they always included her. Florence, the youngest sister, was only six years older than Doreen, and she treated her like her own little sister. For Halloween, Florence dressed Doreen in mama Anna's clothes to go trick or treating. The favorite pastime for the two of them was playing jacks and jumping rope. They were inseparable. I guess we were doing something right. Making Doreen happy was our main goal, and happy she was.

When summertime came around again we all went to Jersey. This time, we took Anna and Florence along with us. It was like old home week. Just about all of the same vacationers were there again. Our friend John was there with a new girlfriend. She was Swedish and spoke very little English, but all the women enjoyed her company and friendship. All in all it was one of the best summers ever. The only drawback was that we couldn't stay longer than a week. All the guys had to get back to work, and John was leaving for India right after the vacation. Around the campfire one evening, he told us that traveling overseas was beginning to get very dangerous. His family had a home in England, but he wouldn't be going there that year because they were considering coming to New York to live as soon as possible. It seemed that Adolph Hitler was getting ready to form an alliance with Benito Mussolini.

Hitler and his psycho gang were invading Poland, Denmark, and Norway and had their eyes on France, Italy, and the United Kingdom. John didn't think that it was just a rumor, because he had received correspondence from other members of his family who lived in some of those countries.

What the hell was going on in Europe? And what was Mussolini thinking? Going in with Hitler? That was insane. If this was true, how far would it go? We left New Jersey on a solemn note. I told John to be very careful on his journeys and to please keep us informed about his parents.

During the fall months, Rose started taking Doreen to dance lessons. She was learning ballet and tap. I couldn't believe those little feet were actually dancing. I mean really dancing. When I came home from work at night, she danced around the rooms and we all joined in the fun. My two girls were a joy to behold. This was family. This was living and loving. What else could a man ask for?

Well, two things were still bothering me. First, where were my kid brothers? And second, what if President Roosevelt decided to get into the European dilemma? Lou never wrote much about where he was and what, if anything, he knew. He was just a kid having the adventure of his life. Mike took his Navy life the same way as Lou. Great. Ok. So if there was anything going on they wouldn't seem so cheerful. Right? Right. Gene, Sam, Paul, and Angelo felt the same as me. And yet, what if? It got so we couldn't wait to hear from John. Month after month there was no news from John. That worried me. It just wasn't like him not to keep in touch.

Chapter 36

In November we received a big surprise. Our mama's sister, Aunt Jeanette, had found Sam and called him. I never found out how that happened, but it was good news. Sam said that she was living in Connecticut and had a daughter named Phyllis. Her husband had died suddenly, and she wanted to see mama but didn't know where she was. When Sam told her about mama, pop, and all of us she was shocked. She said that she had never been notified. She went on and on about how sorry she was for all of us and said that we must get together. Sam told her that we would be visiting mama for Christmas and that she was welcome to come with us. She loved the idea so much that she cried. Of course, she would have to get back to Sam because she still had some estate settling to do. Sam was so excited when he talked to her that he forgot to get her address or phone number. My brother Sam had always been the most confident, take no crap, leader of the pack. But this time? I don't know. Maybe I was just being overly suspicious. I was always the doubting Thomas of the family anyway. I just didn't feel comfortable with this sudden revelation.

Poor Sam. God love him. I didn't have the heart to tell him what I had been feeling about Aunt Jeanette, especially since it was now Christmas, and he hadn't heard another word from her. We had a nice visit with mama despite our disappointment in her sister. Look, sometimes you just have to take the good with the bad and make due with what you have. We were a loving and growing family, mama was still with us and happy with our visits, and life was good in every way. These were the good things in our lives. They meant more than getting upset over an aunt who never really cared for us anyway. Once again we left mama with heavy hearts. Sam was furious about the aunt and wanted to find Tony and Phil more then ever.

Sam thought that maybe it was time to backtrack and start from the beginning. That sounded plausible. What else could we do? Maybe the new year would bring a change for the good. It was worth a try. It had been a long time, since 1927, since we had been separated. What if the two kids weren't even in New York anymore? Thirteen years is a long time. Boy we could have used some intervention right about now from "the big man."

Chapter 37

In February of 1941, Sam decided to make a visit to our orphanage. That wasn't an easy thing for him to do. He still had memories that he could never get out of his head. I could see the anger and despair he was feeling about going back to that place, especially alone. I told him to wait until I could get a day off from work, but he was determined to get right to it. I should have taken off because I was a nervous wreck all day waiting to hear from him. When I got home from work, I went to his apartment but Vinnie said she hadn't heard from him all day. I was really anxious. What if he had blown up and caused some kind of a commotion at the orphanage? I couldn't eat my dinner and Rose suggested that I call Gene, so that and he and I could go looking for Sam. Good idea. I was just calling Gene, when there was a knock at the door. I held my breath as I went to see who it was. I prayed it wasn't the police about Sam.

Standing there with a silly grin on his face was Sam. I pulled him into the apartment, sat him on the sofa, and said "Speak. What happened? Are you in trouble?" The son of a gun just laughed till he had tears in his eyes. Finally, he started telling me the wildest story ever. He had arrived at the orphanage about 10:00 a.m. and went straight to the head office. When he told them who he was and why he was there, they held him up for an hour proving his identity, social number, drivers license, and the names of his parents, his brothers, and on and on, till he was nearing his melting point. Then they finally started going through all of our records for another hour. And there it was, right in front of him. Every one of us had been accounted for including Tony and Phil. They were located almost immediately, and guess where they were? Yep, right there. The two boys had been bounced around over and over again until they ended up right where they were on that horrible day thirteen years ago. Talk about luck though. They had only been there for the past two months. If only we had known at Christmas. Well Sam knew now and he wanted to see them right away.

Sam spent the next three hours with Tony and Phil. Their first sight of each other was heartbreaking. The kids had no idea who Sam was, and if Sam had passed them on the street, he would not have known them. When he introduced himself to them, he explained that there were seven of us, and that we had all been separated and had been searching for each other, and them, for years. He also told them that we had never given up looking for them, and we had a chance to be a whole family again. Of course, it was up to them. We had always wanted them back in our lives and we wanted them to make their own choices. He said he knew it must have been frightening for them to suddenly meet this total stranger who says they have not one, but five brothers waiting for them to come home. Sam told me it was amazing sitting there and talking with them. They were practically men now. Tony was a tall, skinny, fourteen-year-old, and Phil was a little shorter, muscular, thirteen-year-old. They both had the dark hair like papa. Tony was the shy, quiet one, and Phil was the happy, chatty one. They asked a thousand questions about mama and papa and each of their brothers. They were never told that they had a family.

They had always thought that they were unwanted orphans. They didn't even know that they themselves were brothers until a few years ago. Tony didn't want to have a brother to be responsible for, but Phil turned out to be the one kid there who didn't need protection; he was tough as steel. It took them a long time to become friendly with one another. But they did, and there they were with an older brother they would have to learn to like. Wow, seven brothers. It suddenly started to sound like a good thing was about to happen.

When Sam had to leave, he asked them if we could all have a few visits with them to get to know one another. It would give them a chance to see for themselves what lay ahead. Both boys agreed to meet with us and wanted it to be as soon as possible. I couldn't wait. I wanted to see them as soon as possible. My brothers. Oh God, I couldn't believe it. Our prayers had finally been answered. They were alive and well and going to be coming home again, and the sooner the better. I thought, "Mama they're coming to you."

We started seeing the boys the following week, and for three weeks it was torture for all of us. The poor kids didn't know what to make of us. They had no recollections of their lives before the orphanage. Our faces meant nothing to them and our stories even less. I could tell Tony was a little leery of us, but Phil seemed eager to get out of there and have a family. I hoped that they weren't having feelings of resentment towards us for not finding them sooner. I explained, as best I could, how we had been looking for them for years, and how much we needed them in our lives. I also told them that mama kept asking for them, and was growing impatient with us for not bringing them to see her. Finally there was a break through. Phil asked if there was any way for us to take them to see mama.

We jumped at the chance. Sam ran right into the office and got permission for Tony and Phil to spend a weekend with him.

For the next couple of months, Sam had the kids every other weekend. We all got together on those weekends and were growing closer all the time. Our first visit with them to see mama was unbelievable. Tony had a real smile on his face. Something in him brought out a faint enough memory of mama to finally make him believe we were his family. Phil was just plain happy to be a part of us. And mama. She hugged and kissed them so much they were overwhelmed. How she knew they were her babies was beyond me. But she did, and we were happy for the boys and for mama. She finally had seen all seven of her sons and knew that they were all right.

Next we had to get custody of them. We also had to arrange where they would live and with whom. It was already the middle of 1941, and we wanted them out of that orphanage ASAP. Since none of our apartments were big enough to house two, almost adult young men, Sam and I came up with an idea agreed upon by all. There was an apartment available right between my apartment and Sam's. They could have their own apartment, and both Sam and I would be close enough to keep an eye on them. The kids loved that idea and preferred new sleeping arrangements, because they were sick of living with a hundred other boys. Before we could set them up, we had to finalize our custody papers. With that done, the boys moved in to their new home. We had found our brothers and were now a complete family.

Chapter 38

When summer rolled around, we were all anxious for some family fun and relaxation. We all, including Tony and Phil, headed for our hideaway in New Jersey.

John called to say that he was finally home and would meet us at the resort. Doreen had her tonsils removed in June, and was as fit as a fiddle in time for our vacation. A little too fit as it turned out. She was a dynamo in constant motion. Anna, Florence, Tony and Phil, all being teenagers, were assigned as adult playmates to all the little kids for one hour each morning. They had the kids playing so much and so hard that nap time couldn't come soon enough for the little tykes. A good time was being had by all. We adults swam, played games, and had our own fireside chats just like President Roosevelt had. When we asked John what he knew, he said that he didn't want to talk about his travels until after the children were asleep.

On the second afternoon of our stay in Jersey, Rose and I were both tucking Doreen in for her nap when we declared our plans for the future. Having loved the quiet, peaceful surroundings of the resort, we decided it was time to start making plans for a home in the suburbs of New York. I told Rose that Mr. Ludlam was looking into building homes on Long Island by the next year. That sounded good to both of us, and right then and there we set our goal on buying a house in the suburbs. It was great to know that we were always on the same page. We hugged and kissed, kissed Doreen sweet dreams, and went to tell our friends and family of our plans for the very near future. Half an hour later, our happy plans turned to unspeakable terror.

While all of the kids were supposed to be napping, Doreen had decided to go for a swim in the lake. Not just a swim but a jump from the high diving board. All of the adults were sitting around the campfire when Rose screamed out that Doreen was at the edge of the diving board. I jumped up started screaming for Doreen not to move and ran to the lake.

I was waving my arms and screaming like a madman. Doreen must have thought I was happy to see her and running to join her because just as I got to the edge of the shoreline, she jumped. Fear gripped my soul as I plunged into the water. I swam to the area of the diving board and dove in. I came up for air and just as I was about to dive again, I saw her little legs paddling and her arms pushing at the water. Damn if she wasn't swimming and heading for the beach. I rushed to her and scooped her into my arms. She was giggling and happy as a lark. I was crying and happy she was alive. By the time we got to the beach, everybody was waiting at the water's edge. Most of the men were in the water, right behind us. I never even realized that I was not alone in my flight to rescue Doreen. Gene, Sam, John and my brothers were right there with me all along. There was a guardian angel watching over us that day.

Chapter 39

That night, after dinner, the women decided to stay close to the cabins and play cards. After some time playing horseshoes, we guys sat around the campfire. I could tell John had something on his mind. He was pretty quiet since he arrived at the resort and had never once mentioned anything about his latest travels. When all of the women and children went off to bed, John asked me to stay outside for awhile. Gene, Sam, Angelo, Rocco, and Paul joined us. John was very upset about what was happening in Europe. Although we had heard some of the goings on over there from the movie newsreels, radio, and newspapers, what he told us put a fear in each of us. Hitler's Nazi party had taken over the German government, and since January of 1940 he had invaded Poland, Denmark, and Norway. Hitler had formed an alliance with Mussolini of Italy against France and the United Kingdom. England then started its own attacks against the Nazis in Norway.

Some of John's family was trying to get to America while other family members were joining England's military. John was going back to England to join the RAF as soon as he could get his family settled in America. We were all in a state of shock and despair. Hearing these stories from someone who had actually seen it all first hand was quite different from what we'd heard in the news. I thought, "God help John, England, and maybe us."

How could Mussolini have united with Hitler? What did that say for all Italians? And what was Hitler after? "World possession," John said. John felt that Hitler was maniacal enough to try and conquer as many countries as possible starting with Europe. His theory sounded impossible. Germany was just a small country. John said that if Hitler started getting anymore allies, nothing was impossible. The Germans had already started mass executions in Poland, and after invading Amsterdam, Northern France, Brussels, and Belgium those countries were already surrendering. England's new Prime Minister, Winston Churchill, had his hands full and was begging for support.

There was a moment of silence from all of us. It was as though the grim reaper had just brushed against everyone at this telling. I knew we all had the same thoughts running through our heads. Will America get involved and how do we not get into it? We told John that we all understood how he felt about his family and their ancestral home. Although he was an American citizen, his duty was understandably to his family and the country of their ancestral heritage. Our prayers were with him and we would always be there for him. And then Gene started asking John questions about the RAF. Were they taking American volunteers, and how did one go about signing up? Angelo and Paul joined in with the same questions.

I looked at Sam and knew at once that he was thinking the same thoughts as me. Would we have to leave our wives and children to go off to war? Could our families be safe at home without us? Did we have the right to get into a war that didn't involve us? We knew the answers without even voicing them. Yes!! John seemed to be reading our thoughts. He told us that no one in their right minds doubted the strength and loyalties of the people of the United States. If push came to shove, the people of America would show their power to suppress any proposed annihilation of this country and our neighbors around the world. The United States has never backed down in the fight for liberty. We had to wait on the decision of President Roosevelt.

Sleep was totally out of the question that night. I clung to Rose with all the love in me. I watched Doreen sleeping so peacefully in her bed, but could not defeat the fear in my heart of what might be lying in wait for us. On that night, I vowed to protect my family in any and every way necessary. If it meant going to war, then so be it. I knew that I would have to tell Rose what John had discovered on his trip to Europe. I didn't want to frighten her, but she had to know the truth of what was happening and what might still lie ahead. I had no idea how she would take this information, or even if this threat was an omen of what might be. After all, this misery in Europe had been going on for years. Of course, it had escalated but this was already the middle of 1941, and there were no obvious signs that America might get involved. With England showing its strengths it would probably be over soon anyway. England was a powerful country too, and like America, it would fight for its rights against any country led by a degenerate like Hitler. However, I had to concentrate on the present.

Doreen was starting school in September and Rose was thinking of going back to work. Our future was secure and I wanted to keep it that way.

Chapter 40

President Roosevelt gave a chilling, fireside chat on September 11, 1941. What he said added to the doubts and questions I had been mulling over ever since our talk with John. FDR spoke of our U.S. destroyer *Greer,* which had been torpedoed twice by a German submarine. Apparently, there had been other attacks on American vessels in Atlantic ocean waters. A merchant ship, the Robin Moor, was sunk by a Nazi submarine. Another merchant ship, the Steel Seafarer, was sunk by a German aircraft in the Red Sea. Our President was outraged that the Hitler government was acting in defiance of the laws of the sea in an attempt to seize control of the oceans. He also said that Hitler and his plots to sabotage the world were all known to the government of the United States. FDR concluded his chat with a warning to German and Italian vessels of war that when they enter the waters that America protects, they do so at their own peril. He likened the Nazi submarines and raiders to "Rattlesnakes of the Atlantic." I remember his words, "When you see a rattlesnake poised to strike, you do not wait until he has struck before you crush him." Here, Here Mr. President. That's telling them. Amen to that.

That fireside chat left my veins icy. John wasn't kidding when he said that the Nazi's were trying to take over the world. Crazy thoughts were running around in my brain. How far will they go before we were pulled into the fight? Time would tell. The whole world seemed to be suddenly spinning out of control. Even Japan, the third largest Naval force in the world, behind the United States and England, was taking cues from Hitler. Japan was taking over countries like China, Korea and European colonies in Asia.

Emperor Hirohito of Japan was building a large and modern Navy and militarizing his country with such a rapid industrialization that it needed resources not available on the Japanese homelands. Thus, they invaded the lands that had the resources that Japan needed. I thought, " God help us if they allied with Germany and Italy."

Chapter 41

September had passed and all was well in America. My little family was doing just great. Doreen loved school and Rose found a job she liked in a book bindery. Our friend and neighbor, Adele, who had two little girls of her own watched Doreen from 3:00 to 4:30 when Rose came home from work. We were all happy with our new lifestyle. I started working in Long Island building homes and the money was coming in nice and steady. Rose and I were already picturing our little house in the suburbs with a white picket fence and a huge fireplace for the winter months. Although I had told Rose what John had told me of the strife in Europe, I never mentioned to her that he had left for England to join the RAF. When our weekends ended up with all the guys huddled in a corner chattering away, she just assumed we were either talking about our jobs or the Brooklyn Dodgers.

After Thanksgiving we started making plans for the Christmas visit to see mama. Sam had never heard from Aunt Jeanette again and pop was long forgotten. We received letters from Mike and Lou stating that they couldn't get leave that Christmas. According to them, life was great and all was well. Mike was near some Islands off the Atlantic Ocean, and Lou's ship was moored in Hawaii for maintenance work. It sounded good. News from them was never very enlightening, but it was good to know that they were doing well. John surprised us by coming home at the end of November.

John looked haggard and restless. He didn't say much about where he'd been and what, if anything, he'd seen or heard lately. All he said was that his parents were settled in an apartment in Manhattan, and that he'd had a very bad setback with pneumonia.

When he left I had to assume that I wouldn't be seeing him for a long time. His embraces and sad eyes said a mountain of unspoken words. I thought, "He must be leaving for England. God speed good friend, stay safe, and come home to us soon."

Chapter 42

On Sunday morning, December 7, 1941, we went to church and headed for mama Anna's for our usual family get-together. Everybody was having a great time playing with the kids, and eating everything in sight, when Rose's sister Lena came running in from the parlor. She was the quiet sister who never made waves and just enjoyed sitting around while we told stories, or she'd be off listening to the radio in the parlor. Well on that day Lena was hysterically crying and yelling for us to go inside and listen to the radio. The poor kid was beside herself, and we couldn't imagine what she'd heard on the radio. In one fell swoop, the entire family was huddled around the radio listening to an unbelievable broadcast. The announcer was crying and trying to blurt out the news of a disaster in Hawaii. As he regained his composure, we were all weeping at what he was telling all of America.

At 7:20 a.m. Pacific time the Island of Oahu in Hawaii was hit with a wave of Japanese airplanes from aircraft carriers out at sea. Our Naval fleet consisting of destroyers and numerous other ships were being bombed and sunk right there in the harbor. By 9:30 a.m. Pacific time the Island itself was under attack. Our planes never had a chance to get in the air, and our ships were scrambling to get under way in the besieged harbor. Thousands of Americans were being killed by this surprise attack. Japan had declared war on the United States. Everyone in the room looked at me and Sam and said nothing, as tears ran down their cheeks. We were all of one mind at that moment. Lou, Mike, and America. I took Sam's hand as the pain in my gut wrenched my very soul. Our brothers. "Oh dear God, they're just two kids trying to grow up. Now they've been thrown right in the middle of a war with only one way out." My silent prayer went up to a merciful Christ. " Please protect my brothers and bring them home safely to us, and may all of our fallen Americans find peace and salvation in your arms."

For the next couple of days, the death toll in Hawaii kept rising. Stories of tragedy and heroism floated across the radio airwaves. At least 2,390 deaths were recorded thus far. One radio broadcast hit Sam and I like a bombshell. The USS Nevada had been damaged during the bombardment, and while heading to open sea it saw the USS Arizona go down in a huge fireball. It was doubtful that there were any survivors. Sam said that Lou had mentioned the name of the ship he was on, but it was a while back and Sam just wasn't sure. I tried to remember if Lou had said Arizona or Nevada. At one time, Lou had said it was funny that he was assigned to a ship with the name of the state he wanted to live in.

Chapter 43

On December 8, President Roosevelt confirmed our fears in his speech to Congress. He started his speech by calling December 7, 1941 "a date which will live in infamy." FDR went on to say that, "the premeditated invasion by Japan, and the danger to our country leaves no choice but to declare a state of war between the United States and the Japanese empire." So, there we were. Suddenly, our futures were hanging in the balance. There was no way we Americans would not fight back. Japan had made a big mistake.

They didn't know how powerful we could be when united against oppression of any kind. As far as I was concerned, my wife and daughter were never going to be hurt as long as I lived, and I had planned on living a long time for them. Rose knew exactly how I felt, and although there was fear in her heart she realized what had to be done. There were no words to be said, no speeches to be made, and what would be, would be. It was all in the name of life and liberty. This was our country, and by God we would keep it that way.

I thought to myself, "Look, I'm no hero or some kind of a political nut, but I do love my country. America has given us every opportunity for a good life. We are blessed, happy, and thankful for what we have or can still have in the future. Besides, with the chance of invasion on our home soil looming over us as a possibility, my gut feeling, and that of everyone I know, is to get moving as fast as we can to "hold the fortress by all means, so to speak." Our friend John's dilemma was now quite obvious. Without another word from him, we understood the torment he'd been going through. Whoever said, "United we stand, divided we fall" sure was telling it as it is. As it turned out, our problem with Japan was just the beginning.

Three days later, on December 11 Nazi Germany and Fascist Italy declared war on the United States. Well, if that didn't cut the cake. Hitler, Mussolini, and Hirohito all palsy walsy. So there we stood with war from the Pacific and war from the Atlantic. Ok. Did the unholy trio forget that we were not the only ones who wanted to see them all defeated? All we had to do now was start production on military equipment, and develop an Army like never before seen in the history of man. That was a big, hurry-up order to fill. Every American man and woman was already getting ready for their call to arms. We knew we could do it. And we would do it.

The next few weeks were a scramble with patriots from all over the states signing up immediately, and getting into the production of military equipment. Since all of the able-bodied men were joining the armed services, women and men who couldn't make the call were becoming our tools of production. Security measures were set into motion. Eyes and ears were on the beaches, at the ports, at all the waterways, every possible entryway into America and in the skies. In the homes, schools, stores, and wherever there were windows, dark curtains were arranged to be closed at night in case of an air raid. Subways and underground passages were selected for shelter in the event of an attack. We were ready. That was our message to the world, and now our messages to our families were next.

Chapter 44

We called for a family gathering the following Sunday. We men knew, and the women knew, that this wasn't going to be our usual Sunday happy time; it was going to be a declaration of intentions day. There was no hidden agenda. Everyone knew what to expect. At home, Rose and I talked about what was the best road for me to take, and when to take it. Should I sign up right away or wait for the inevitable draft? There was absolutely no question of my staying out of the war. Rose feared but understood my need. She put up a brave front promising to make sure that she and Doreen would be safe, and that I would be in her dreams every night, and her thoughts every day. That's when it hit me. I had always promised my angel that nothing would ever keep us apart again, and now I was going to break that promise. I thought, "Please God, tell me that I'm doing the right thing for my two angels."

There was no crying or arguments when we had our Sunday family meeting. Our women were the backbone of America. All the men had talked to their wives before Sunday, so there were no surprises. The women had talked amongst themselves and had decided to stand by each of their men. They weren't happy about our decision, but they understood. One by one, we guys spoke of our decisions. Gene was the first. He said that he would be joining the Marines in January. His wife Inez and their children, Doris and Bart, would be staying with Inez's mother and sister. Sam was next. His choice was the Army. Vinnie and their children, Theresa and Bobby, would be staying at their apartment so that Tony and Phil could be near them. I was next. I looked at Gene and told him that I was headed for the Marines too. His face lit up like a Christmas tree and he gave me a big hug. I told him he'd be going before, me because Sam and I had to make sure everything with Tony and Phil was secure by February. Rose and Doreen would be staying with mama Anna and the girls. Paul took the floor next and said he wanted to go into the Army but he had a problem. He had been dating a girl, Louise, for a while now and didn't know what to do about her. We all laughed and Gene told him to write her every day, and if she doesn't get tired of his letters, then he'd know what to do. Rocco thought he might be too old (he was nearing forty) to be accepted into the Army, but he was going to try anyway. Angelo said he was glad that he didn't have a girlfriend because he was going into the Army and would find a nice Italian girl when we conquered Italy.

Mary's boyfriend Sal had come to dinner also. He hadn't said a word until we were all finished. He stood up very slowly and walked over to mama Anna. He sat next to her and held her hand. "Mama" he said "I think you know how much I love your daughter Mary." Mama just nodded yes and smiled her beautiful smile. She wasn't going to make this easy for him. "Mama, I would like your permission to get engaged to Mary right away. In fact, I would like to ask her right now." Mama squeezed his hand and said that if Mary was in love with him, she would not object to his proposal. So right then and there, in front of the whole family, Sal got down on one knee in front of Mary, took a ring out of his jacket pocket, and begged Mary to marry him. Of course, she said yes and that she would plan her wedding for when he came home from the Army. Sal said that as soon as the war was over, and he was sure it wouldn't be too long, he promised she would have the biggest wedding ever.

As we were all getting ready to go home mama Anna stopped us and said " I feel in my heart that Jesus will be watching over all of you. He will keep you safe because he loves you, and knows how much I love all my boys. Oh, and Angelo, when you conquer Italy and have Mussolini in front of you, tell him that America's Italians are ashamed of him, and that God will not forgive him for doing the devil's work. " So that was the way that day ended. Our futures were in God's hands after all.

Chapter 45

Christmas 1941. Not a great year for celebrating peace on earth when the whole world was being turned inside out. Our visit with mama was a disaster too. She was having a bad week, and we didn't get much visiting time with her. We had three cars; we had Gene's, Sam's and now my car, filled with family and friends who wanted to see mama now in case of the possible long time between visits. We all tried to make the most out of the Holidays, but there was a pall hanging over all of us. Well, maybe happy New Year? We all prayed for that.

By the middle of January, Gene had grown impatient and he and three buddies enlisted. Gene told me he'd be in Camp Lejeune waiting for me, and that I should be ready to take orders from him because he was going to be pushing for non-com officer. I hated the thought of him leaving without me, but February was right around the corner and then I'd meet up with him, non-com or not. My boss, Mr. Ludlam, had heard about construction units being put together for the Navy. I told him I wanted to be a Marine and not a sailor. He said the units were not officially in the Navy, but just working for them. I appreciated his concern. I knew that he thought that if I were in construction I wouldn't be fighting. He had become more like a father to me than a boss. But, I was determined to be a Marine.

I finally received a short note from John. He had joined the RAF, but was stuck doing office work because his bout with pneumonia had left him with some physical problems. He didn't say where he was nor did he give any specifics about his duties. I knew in my heart that a man with his intelligence and world knowledge was not just a secretary. I felt quite certain that he was in a vital position of the defense of England. There was no forwarding address, so I couldn't let him know what was going on with all of us at home. I hoped I would hear from him before I left. I stopped by his apartment one day while I was in Manhattan. This was the first time I'd met his parents. They were as charming and well versed as John. They had also received a short note from John and were worried about him. I told them not to worry because John was a good man with an angel on his shoulder. When I left them, I looked to the heavens and prayed that I was right about that angel.

A week after Gene left for boot camp Paul, Angelo, and Sal enlisted in the army. The tears were flowing like crazy throughout the family.

All the red tape for Tony and Phil to stay out of the home while Sam and I were gone was holding us up from enlisting. My neighbor friends Jim and Angelo had already joined the Army and were at boot camp. All the men we knew were somewhere out there getting prepared to fight or had shipped out.

Chapter 46

I had a job at the stockyards I was finishing up when I saw a poster that caught my eye. It said "Build for your Navy. Enlist! Carpenters, Machinists, Electricians, etc. U.S. Bureau of Yards and Docks." So this must be what Mr. Ludlam had been telling me about. I decided to stop at the recruiting office on the way home to get some information about this construction deal.

It was a very interesting bit of info I picked up. Apparently, in March of that year (1942), Rear Admiral Morell had gained approval from the Bureau of Navigation to recruit men from the construction trades for assignment to a Naval regiment. Construction battalions had been created and they were named Seabees. Their function was to build roads, airfields, bridges etc. in war zones. They would not only be doing necessary construction, but would be weapon-carrying defenders as well. Wow, right up my alley. I would get to fight for my country and use my construction skills to protect and advance our service men. This, I had to do. I signed up right then and there. I would be leaving for basic training in three weeks, so I had to get everything at home in order right away. My emotions were running wild I was happy because I was finally getting my chance to fight. I was also sad at the thought of leaving my girls for who knew how long. I was scared; sure I was afraid of never coming home again or maybe even being badly wounded. I was apprehensive in thinking how I would I handle the sights of war? I had to take first things first. I had to get home right away.

When I arrived at the door to our apartment, I stopped short. What the hell did I do? I enlisted without even telling Rose first. How do I tell my wife and daughter that I'll be leaving in just three weeks? I leaned against the door as tears rolled down my cheeks. I was about to break my promise to Rose and God that we would never be separated again. My head was telling me that this was the right thing to do, but my heart was breaking. I backed away from the door and went up to the roof to sort things out. How do I break the news to my angels? I sat on the ledge for a while still not getting any answers. Finally, I stood up, squared my shoulders, and told myself to start acting like the man my girls loved.

I figured that the news wouldn't be exactly a shock to them; after all we all knew that the day was growing near. It's just the way I did it. Well, here goes nothing. I opened the door and went into the apartment.

Both of my girls were setting the table for dinner and when they saw me they came running over with hugs and kisses for me. Of course Doreen was a non-stop chatterbox and gave me full details of her day. We had a happy dinner and relaxed in front of the radio afterwards. While Rose was getting Doreen ready for bed, I started reading the newspaper. To my surprise, there was a column about the Seabees and what they were all about. Rose sat beside me and said that Doreen was ready for her bedtime story. So, I went in to tell her the story of the Princess and the Pea. The last thing she said to me before she fell asleep, was that she knew just how the princess felt because sometimes a little wrinkle in her sheets made her feel the same way. I tucked her in and gave her a kiss on her forehead. I was thinking that the one thing I wanted more than anything else might never be.

I wanted to be there for her through her growing years . How could that happen now? Rose was sitting on the sofa with the newspaper on her lap when I came out of the bedroom. I took a deep breath, sat down beside her, and put my arm around her shoulders. Rose put her head on my chest and said, "Did you sign up today?" I nearly fell off the sofa. How did she always know what I had done before I even got to open my mouth? She said that after reading the article about the Seabees, she knew that I would jump at the chance to join a construction outfit. What could I say? She hit the nail right on the head.

I told her about my day, where I had gone, and what I wound up doing. My angel snuggled up to me and told me that she was not surprised at my decision, and that she was ready also. We discussed the plans for my departure, the household expenses, and how to tell Doreen. Rose said that Doreen had been asking if I would be leaving too when she saw all the men in our family going away to war. Rose had assured her that I too would be a soldier, and that she could write to me every day. How lucky could a guy be? An angel for a wife and a princess for a daughter. I thought, " Oh, I'll be coming home alright, that's for sure. Nothing will ever take me away again."

A week before I was to leave, Sam had finalized the custodial care for Tony and Phil. Vinnie would be there for them when Sam enlisted. I asked the boys to send me a letter once in a while because I would really be missing them. As it turned out, Sam was rejected when he went to enlist. The doctors had found a slight heart problem and a punctured eardrum. Sam would be staying home making sure our soldiers were getting the supplies and equipment they needed to stay alive and win the war.

I knew my big brother's heart was breaking because he had always been a fighter and he wanted to fight for his country and family. I loved Sam and understood what he was feeling, but secretly I was relieved to know that at least three of my brothers would be safe at home and if the rest of us never came back they would keep the family roots in tact.

Chapter 47

The years 1942 to 1945 were the worst years of my life. Nothing before this time could compare to what was happening in my life at that time. Construction on hot, bug-infested little Islands, and surrounded by Japanese snipers, pierced my soul with memories better left unspoken. Enduring the heartache of being thousands of miles away from my two angels was unbearable. The not knowing how my family was getting along, and whether or not they were completely safe from the monsters who were terrorizing the world, was a heavy burden to bear. But I was not alone in my pain. I knew that every American soldier in every corner of the fighting world was having the same feelings. The life and death horrors of war were devastating to the soul. There was just no place like home and family, especially when any day could be your last day.

But we persevered. Every skirmish strengthened our determination to bring the enemy to their knees. Letters and packages from home gave us temporary comfort and a warming of the heart. My girls and our family were safe. That was all that mattered to me. A close brush with death empowered my will to live and get home as quickly as possible. The fighting went on and on. Getting home seemed like a hopeless dream after awhile. But thanks to the strength of my fellow Americans, it was finally over. The war was declared a victory for the United States and its allies. It was over and we were going home My angels would be in my arms once more.

Chapter 48

Coming home was a mixed bag of emotions. The yearning I had endured for four years was about to be gratified. Rose was more gorgeous than ever, and Doreen had grown into a beautiful young girl. I had missed so much of their lives. It kind of scared me, because I didn't know if we could pick up where we'd been before I'd walked into hell. All that I had experienced in the war years was a haunting I could not dismiss. Will I ever be able to forget? Was I still the same man who went away so many years ago?

Unfortunately during my first few months back home, I walked around with scars on my soul. My girls were great. They showered me with love and attention every day. But my nights were filled with tormenting nightmares. I felt like a stranger in a world I had vowed never to leave again. I thought, " Who am I now?" I prayed for peace of mind and the return of the old Joe Bones. I knew I was headed for disaster, but I didn't know how to stop it. And then Gene finally came home.

We were all at mama Anna's house for Sunday dinner when Gene asked me to take a ride with him to the store for some soda. When we pulled up to the store, he asked me to wait a minute, he wanted to talk about something. He said that Rose had called him because she was worried about me. I told him what was going on in my head, and that I didn't know what to do about it. He said that he and all the guys he knew were going through the same thing. We would all be scarred for life, but we had to learn how to put the war far, far back in our memory bank. We had to live for today and all the tomorrows to come with the loves we had come home to. Some of our buddies didn't make it home, and some came home with severed bodies, or broken homes.

"Look Joe, we were the lucky ones. We came home alive and in one piece to our loved ones. We're still young with a lifetime of happiness ahead for us. Scars have a way of fading after a while if we push them aside and concentrate on the future. Nobody knows what tomorrow has in store for us, so we live the best way we can for today and share our love with the ones who love us in return. Look, if we could survive World War II we are strong enough to make the best of whatever life may throw our way. Hang in there kid. Just keep reminding yourself how lucky you are to have a wife and daughter who consider you their whole world. And never forget that I love you as my own brother and I will always be there for you. So start living again for Rose, Doreen and yourself."

As usual Gene was right. He was the heart and soul of the family. He was my brother. It was time for me to straighten up, put the past behind me, and give my two angels the best things in life that they deserved. How callous it was of me not to realize that the past four years hadn't been easy for them either. They had been living in fear and dread also having to face alone the blackouts, the reports of fallen friends and neighbors, and me not there to comfort them. What an ass I was. They managed to get through it, and, I had to do the same. I thought, "Sorry my loves Joe is back, and I promise to stop thinking of the past and concentrate only on our future together from now until the day I die." When Gene and I got back to dinner, he made an announcement that floored the whole family. His new career was as a Marine. He had reenlisted. As mama Anna wiped a tear from her eye she said, "Thank God there is no more war."

Chapter 49

We all agreed to that statement. But with Gene gone, war or not, it was like having my brother taken away from me again. Gene was preparing to leave in two weeks to arrange for housing for Inez and their kids. He had made sergeant and would now be teaching young recruits how to be the best there was. I promised Gene and Inez that once they were all settled in Rose, Doreen, and I would come for a visit. Mama Anna said, "You squeeze me in the car too?" We all laughed and put the sadness of his leaving again momentarily behind us for the rest of the day. All of a sudden, Paul jumped up and announced that he and Louise wanted to get married before Gene left. It was short notice, he said, but she had been ready for four years. Mary who was sitting next to mama started to whimper on mama's shoulder. Sal hadn't come home yet, and she was worried sick. Mama put her arms around Mary and told her that he would be home soon. Mama felt his return in her heart. Mary never lost faith in her love for Sal, and knew he would keep his promise to marry her. It was just that everybody else was either home or at least on their way home, so where was he? The last she'd heard was that he was somewhere in Africa. Gene told Mary to be patient, and that he would be home soon. I told her that Angelo, our friend John, and our two neighbor friends Angelo and Jim were also not home yet. And as for my brothers Mike and Lou, their ships were still somewhere out on the high seas. I said "God is sending them all back to us real soon. After all, somebody has to clean up after the mess your gung-ho brother Gene left behind." Time heals all wounds and I was sure counting on that right then.

Gene gave me a playful punch and we started sparring around the room. Everyone brightened up after our silly display.

Tony and Phil had become young men while I was away. They had good jobs and their own apartments now. Unfortunately, living together had not been the best thing.

Living apart was much better for their relationship. Living close to Sam and his overly protective nature was tantamount to an explosion waiting to happen. The boys stayed in constant contact with Sam anyway. They spent every Sunday with Sam and his family, and every night Sam dropped by their apartments to check up on them. They were good kids and never caused any trouble. Tony was still very shy, but Phil connected with people easily. Sam made sure they visited mama every Easter and Christmas. She was slipping into short comas now, and Sam urged us all to see mama as often as possible. Angelo and Mike had finally come home and were ready for life. Lou made the Navy his career choice and was still on the seas. So now we were six brothers visiting mama. Our lives were moving along so fast it seemed that time had suddenly gone into overdrive.

Chapter 50

The year 1946 brought a lot of changes to all of us. I couldn't believe that Rose and I were now celebrating our tenth anniversary. After five years in the Army, Sal finally came home and he and Mary had a beautiful wedding. Paul and Louise were having their first child, and Gene and his family were now stationed in Virginia. Jenny and her family were still living on Second Avenue in Manhattan, and Lena, Anna, and Florence were still living with mama Anna. Mike married a girl, Millie, from the neighborhood, and Angelo and his wife Anne were living in Corona. Lou made it home once a year and only he, Tony, and Phil were the unmarried ones.

Rose and I had both been working and socking the money away for our Long Island home-to-be. We started taking our New Jersey vacations at White Hall Manor again with the same friends and relatives from those first years. This particular summer was a little rough on Rose though.

She came down with some stomach problems. She couldn't hold down her food and she fainted a couple of times. She had me worried sick. I wanted to go home right away but she refused saying that she didn't want to ruin Doreen's fun. So, to my surprise, she stuck it out. I couldn't believe how she seemed to recuperate by the time we were home again. Of course, she insisted there was no need to see a doctor after all. It was probably just something she ate at the resort. She went back to work and her stomach problem had disappeared, so she said. Two weeks later, I woke up one night and noticed she wasn't in bed, so I went to find her. She was coming out of the bathroom and told me that she hadn't wanted to tell me that she'd been sick to her stomach for the past two days. Well, that was it. In the morning, we dropped Doreen off at school and went to the doctor's office.

Chapter 51

Miracle or disaster. I wasn't sure how to take it when the doctor told us that we were pregnant again. It had been so many years since her first pregnancy with Doreen. I was not the only one scared. I could see the torment in my angel's eyes. We stopped at the church on our way home. I guess we were of one mind at that point. Did God have a plan for us? Will he be there for Rose and our baby? Father Branco saw us praying and came over to us. He asked if there was something wrong and if he could help us. He listened as we explained our fears to him. He told us if a new life were to enter our world, it would be a blessing from God and the Holy Mother. We must have faith in God's will and in ourselves.

We went to the one person we knew who could understand better than anyone else what we were feeling. Mama Anna. She listened to our whining and held Rose's hand throughout our whole explanation of what the doctor and the priest had told us. Mama Anna said she understood our fears, but it was time to put our fate in God's hands.

She put her hands on Rose's tummy and said a silent prayer. Then she kissed Rose's cheeks and said, "God will have to take care of you and your baby because he will be so busy listening to the prayers from your whole family, that he will know that this is something he must do. Next to God there is nothing stronger than family." I hoped that she was right.

We went back to Doctor Dora. We wondered if she was still at the same office. Luckily, she was at the same office and May was only seven months away. That was when God would have to be at his best. Rose insisted on working for a few more months, but when the weather started getting too nasty I asked her to please stay home. She did, but she kept herself busy getting things ready for the new baby, and showering Doreen with much, more love. She was worried about how Doreen would feel about having a baby come into our lives. Would it be an intrusion? Would she feel neglected? Would there be any jealously? After all, she had been an only child for nine years.

But there was no need to worry. Doreen was excited and couldn't wait to have a little sister or brother. She was so proud to be a big sister. She thought of all the things she could teach the baby, and all the bedtime stories she could tell. I knew that she would never stop being my second love. We were so worried about Doreen that I suddenly asked myself the question, could I ever love another child the way I have loved Doreen? Rose said the love in my heart was boundless and not to worry. I would try. As for that moment in time though, I just didn't see how it could ever be.

I was a walking zombie. I guess I worried more than anybody else. I was so frightened that we might have a repeat of the first pregnancy. Sure, it turned out all right then, but we couldn't go through that experience again. I couldn't be left with the responsibility of saying no to our baby's life. No, not again.

Doctor Dora was confident that this pregnancy was progressing smoothly, and she was keeping a close eye on Rose and the baby.

Chapter 52

April 1947 was coming to an end and Rose started having false labor pains. The doctor said not to worry; Rose would know when the labor pains were real. On the morning of May 3,1947, a beautiful spring day, Mary was at the apartment with Rose when her water broke. An immediate call went out to me and the rest of the family. The labor pains started and they were for real. I made it home in fifteen minutes, which was just in time to catch Rose and Mary getting ready to walk out the door. Like the nervous fool that I was, I hurried them both into the car and made a mad dash for the hospital. Doctor Dora was waiting for us, and rushed Rose into the delivery room. When the doctor came out only an hour later, fear gripped my heart, I was certain that something was wrong again. She put her hands on my shaking shoulders and asked me if I would like to see Rose and our new baby. I couldn't believe it. Rose and the baby were fine. We were given our miracle. I was in such a hurry to see them that I forgot to ask the doctor if we had a boy or a girl.

Rose looked great. She was smiling from ear to ear. "We did just fine this time Joe. They will be bringing the baby in soon." I smothered my angel with hugs and kisses. Thank God she not only had an easy delivery but there were no complications this time. When the nurse came in carrying a little bundle wrapped in bunting, I watched in awe as she

138

settled the baby in Rose's outstretched arms. Rose looked at me and started to laugh. "Well, do you want to see…oh wait a minute, you never asked if our baby is a boy or girl." She held the baby up to me and said "Joe Bones, say hello to your new daughter Eileen Anne." Wow! Another girl. Who could be luckier than me?

Now I had three, beautiful angels to love. I held our baby in my arms for the first time, and was amazed at the difference between her and Doreen. She was plump, bald, and very fair in complexion. She was the complete opposite of Doreen. And yet, little Eileen Anne, although different in coloring, had a face that was a duplicate of Doreen's. Rose asked me to get her home right away because she wanted Eileen's big sister to meet her new baby doll. When I asked the doctor when Rose and the baby could go home, she said the next day would be fine because they were both in such good health. When all the family started coming in, I rushed home to Doreen.

God bless her, what a kid. She was just like her mother. Doreen bounced around the apartment when I gave her the news. She ran to arrange the baby's bassinette and layette. I told her we had plenty of time to set things up. I wanted this night to be just for the two of us. I was determined that from then on I would always give my two daughters their special time with me. But that night it was just me and my angel, Doreen.

I took her to the restaurant she loved. It was an old-fashioned Lithuanian restaurant with food to die for. Doreen was so excited that she couldn't sit still for a moment, and made sure to tell anyone passing by our table that she had a new, baby sister. I was happy that she was happy and I knew that this would make Rose very happy too. We stopped on the way home for warm, jelly donuts filled with ice cream. Doreen wanted to play cribbage before bed and as usual amazed me. Darn if she wasn't good. She made her fifteens as fast as I could. Playing games with my little girl was an inspiration to me. I told her that in a couple of years she'd have Eileen beating me too. She laughed and said that I was the silliest and best father in the whole world.

Doreen looked me square in the eye and said. "Daddy, some day I will really beat you at cribbage, and I won't let you get away with making it look like I won." With that she gave me a big kiss and a warm hug. Could anyone believe this kid? Already she was wise to me. Like mother, like daughter. No one will ever pull the wool over their eyes. I thought, "Well, come what may, I will always try to be the kind of father my sweet angels will always love because I will love them forever."

The next morning Doreen and I brought Rose and the baby home from the hospital. From that day on, Doreen became Eileen's big, protective sister and second mother. There were times when I would see Doreen just sitting along side the bassinette watching Eileen sleep. When I asked her what she was doing, she said that she loved the way Eileen's eyes moved around under her lids, and wondered what she could be dreaming. Rose sat next to Doreen and said that babies dream about all the angel friends they left behind. Eileen was still playing with them in her sleep. Doreen asked why she didn't dream of angels. Rose said that it was because when people start to get older they couldn't remember that far back, but that it didn't mean that the angels ever forget us. They watch over us for all of our life. Doreen said, "That must be true because look how the angels watched over daddy and all my uncles." Listening to those two made my heart swell with love and pride. Eileen chose the right family to be born into.

Chapter 53

When August came around Rose said she was ready to show off our new baby in New Jersey. So, off we all went. It was another year and another great summer. Much to our surprise and delight, Gene and his family were able to come with us. Boy I had sure missed my talks with Gene. We made plans to visit them real soon. Mama Anna would love that.

John had grown some gray hair at his temples and looked thinner than usual. He was happy to see how much our family had grown, and that we were all safely at home again. His parents were already anxious to get back to Britain, but he wanted them to wait a while longer while England was still in the process of restorations. Blitz after blitz had done quite a bit of damage. When we men gathered around the nightly campfire, we spoke in whispers of our war experiences. None of us wanted our wives to know what we'd seen and done. Tony and Phil wanted to hear it all because they were eager to join the military. John said, "Be patient because the world powers are never really ready for peace. What we had done to Hiroshima and Nagasaki has sent reverberations of fear around the world. It's not over yet. There is so much that is changing right here in the United States and on every continent. The threat of nuclear power looms over the world."

When President Roosevelt died soon after being elected for a fourth term our Vice President Harry S. Truman became our thirty-third president. FDR never lived to see our victory over Japan on September 2, 1945.

Chapter 54

Around the world, there were new leaders put into office like Juan Peron of Argentina, Ho Chi Min of North Vietnam, Josip Broz Tito of Yugoslavia, and Nehru of India. There was an insurgence of communism throughout Europe and Asia. By 1946, Russia was spreading its communistic beliefs and taking over countries such as Romania, Bulgaria, Hungary, Poland, East Germany, and had split Korea. The Soviet Union was becoming a threat to the world. It was hard to believe that they had been our allies during the war. I guess they reasoned that after almost being crushed by Germany, they needed to not only protect themselves, but they had to show the world their newfound strengths. Whatever their pursuits, as far as I was concerned it was not over yet. No, not by a long shot. What country wouldn't be scrambling to get its own hands on nuclear power? We sure started something with that knowledge.

It was enough, we all said, "Let's forget about the rest of the world right now and enjoy the wonderful life we'd come home to."

After Sunday dinner and just before the winter holidays, Rose's little sister Flo asked if any of us believed that a real UFO fell in Roswell, New Mexico. Some of us laughed and some of us looked kind of scared. I told Flo that John had just bought a new camera called the Polaroid Land Camera, and was thinking of taking a trip to Roswell the next year. I felt sure that if he found anything like a UFO that he would tell us all about it. Chances were, though, that it was just a hoax. Leave it to John to go mystery fishing. He was always seeking to broaden his horizons. Just for the hell of it, I would've loved to have gone with him. I wondered if maybe someday John would just settle down in one place. Yeah, sure.

Chapter 55

The end of 1947 had brought a lot of changes to our family. Tony and Phil had both joined the Army. Mike and Millie had a baby girl they named Dolores, and Angelo and Anne were expecting a baby the next Spring. Rose, Doreen, and I were delighting in the growth of Eileen, and our Christmas visit with mama was another disappointment. Fifteen minutes into our visit, mama had become so agitated and distressed, that she had to be taken to her room. The doctor told us that she had become so used to her quiet and tranquil life that too many people at one time overwhelmed her. Her health had been deteriorating recently. That had a lot to do with her anxiety. She was scheduled for a hysterectomy after the holidays. We asked if we could be there on the day of her surgery and he said that we could. Poor mama. Why had life given her such a bum steer?

Mama deserved better. Sam, Mike, Angelo, and I were able to see her after her surgery. She looked so tiny and timid in the big hospital bed. When she awoke she gave us all a great big smile and told us how much she loved her sons. All the hugs and kisses we gave her were not enough for us. We wished we could take her home. But that was never to be.

Meanwhile, the rest of the world was in turmoil again. President Truman was trying everything possible to stem the advance of communism in Europe and Asia. He introduced the

Truman Doctrine and was sending military and economic aid to Turkey and Greece in the hope of negating communism's spread. Unfortunately, his efforts led to a dispute between Russia and the United States called a "Cold War." There was no fighting, per se, but a lot of tension over who had the right to do what and where. In the middle of all that, Jewish holocaust survivors sailed for Palestine on a ship called "Exodus." The ship and its 4,500 refugees were stopped from entering the Port of Haifa by the British. The United Nations intervened and partitioned the land of Palestine between the Arabs and the Jews, heralding the settling of Israel. Back in the States, the fear of communism hit Hollywood. Many people in the movie industry were being blacklisted and losing their jobs because they were accused of being communists by a committee headed by Senator McCarthy. What a way to end a year. I wondered how far those tensions would go. War again? And with whom? I didn't even want to go there.

Chapter 56

Happy New Year 1948. There was still a lot of strife in the world, but we here in America were starting to see a bright light at the end of the tunnel. War veterans were healing physically and emotionally. Families were united and growing, and homes in the suburbs were being knocked out one after the other in all shapes and sizes. Thanks to the GI Bill Of Rights veterans were buying homes with the help of the U. S. of A. Rose and I still wanted to buy a house, but she wanted to save a little more money for the furnishings we would need. Since I was now doing most of my work on Long Island, I could keep my eyes open for a house Rose would love. And so, our family was still growing. My brother Angelo was the proud father of a son, Larry, born in April, and Paul handed out cigars too for a baby girl, JoAnn, born in July. Before our vacation in Jersey, Rose and I kidnapped mama Anna, and went to Virginia to see Gene and his family. I say kidnapped, because Lena, Anna, and Flo didn't want mama to go without them. I wish I could have taken them too, but there just wasn't enough room in the car. I promised them that I would get a bigger car and they would come with us on our next trip to Virginia.

I drove non-stop to Virginia while all the females slept. The long hours on the road put them all to sleep and that was the only quiet time of the trip. God love them. They were all so excited to see Gene and his family, and who could blame them? Gene was waiting at the door of his house when we pulled up. Boy, did he look great. He was fit as a fiddle and smiling from ear to ear.

Needless to say, he was stampeded by Rose, mama Anna, and Doreen. I was left to carry Eileen and the luggage. Gene swooped her out of my arms and held her up to the sky. She screeched with delight and instantly fell in love with him, just like everybody else who knew him. He finally gave her up to Inez and turned to me. He said, "Semper Fi" and then saluted me. I saluted him back and we hugged each other. It was great to be with him again.

We could only stay for a couple of days because we had found a house we were interested in and had to get back to complete the deal. We made each day with Gene and his family a time of good memories.

Chapter 57

Mama Anna loved telling her children, and now her grandchildren stories of her life in Sicily as a young girl. Her Virginia trip was no different. I remember one story she told that scared the bejeebers out of everyone. Her story began with her as a little girl.

To get water for her family, she had to go to the well at the center of her village. Because she hadn't gone for the water when her mother had asked her earlier in the day, she had to leave for the well when it was already starting to get dark. When she arrived at the well and was leaning over to retrieve the water, she suddenly heard a strange sound behind her. As she turned, she saw the biggest and ugliest, growling wolf. Now, this was no ordinary wolf. It was standing on its hind legs, had big, red eyes, and was wearing a woolen vest with a watch fob hanging from the vests pocket. She dropped her bucket and started running just as fast as she could. The wolf was so close that she could feel his hot breath on her neck, and his claws grabbing at her jacket. She was screaming all the way home, and hearing her screams, her mother had the front door open so she was able to just run in and slam the door shut. Her mother calmed her down, and she explained what she had just seen. Her mother said that it was a well-known fact that the creature she had seen was the werewolf who lived on the hill near their village.

Many, many years ago there was a big city that once stood where their little village was nestled under the dreadful hill above them. The land was rich with grapes and merchandise of all kinds. The people were happy with their prosperity.

Their only fear was angering the baron who ruled the land. He was a cruel and evil man who found pleasure in tormenting anyone who did not abide by his laws. But life went on in the city until one cold and stormy night. The baron was alone in his castle. All of his servants had gone to a wedding in the village and would not be back until the next morning. He was glad to be rid of them for the night because he considered them ignorant peasants who never did anything right. The baron was alone because he had never found a woman who could care for such an evil man. Sometime around midnight he heard a strange sound in his courtyard and went out to see what it could be. While searching the premises, he was attacked by a strange beast. He could not see exactly what kind of beast this was, but he could feel the animal's teeth sinking deep into his neck. He hit the beast with the lantern he'd been carrying and ran back into the castle. He was able to clean and bandage the wound, but for a week he was feverish and disoriented.

The following month, as the full moon covered the city, a mournful howling could be heard throughout the land. It was coming from the baron's castle. A reign of terror swept over the city for the next twenty years. It was said that the baron turned into a werewolf during the rise of the full moon, and that his change brought on a hunger for human life. The city people began leaving their homes, as more and more of them were being killed. Soon the city and the castle fell into ruin. But the legend lived on. Hearing mama Anna tell that story sure made it sound real. Could it be? Nah! But the children believed. Isn't that the wonder of youth? Sometimes, I felt like the world would be a better place if humanity never aged past twelve years. Children might be more content to play at war than to actually fight a war.

Chapter 58

We found the house of our dreams. It was located in Long Island, only twenty minutes from Manhattan, and nestled in a community of trees and farmland. It was a two-bedroom Cape Cod model with a one-car garage, a semi-finished attic, and a full basement. It was a brick front on a half-acre site, and the second house from the corner of the street. A young couple had bought the house six months ago and because of medical problems had to sell it. The house would be ready to move in to in only two months and $10,000 would get it for us. Rose loved the house and so did Doreen and Eileen. There was a mini shopping center, only two blocks away, with an A&P, pharmacy, Italian pork store, Italian deli, and a gas station. The main road was in the process of being paved and would no longer be a dirt road in a matter of a few months. The land on which this house was now standing had been a potato farm only a year ago. And thus, we would be homeowners for the rest of our lives. Rose and I were floating on air.

The summer of 1948 turned out to be our last visit to White Hall Manor in New Jersey. Not by choice, but because I had a lot of plans for our new home. I knew I was taking on a big job, but it would be worth it for my girls. When we told our vacation friends and family about the plans we had, I was happily surprised to hear that many of our group were also looking into settling in Long Island. That would be the ultimate pleasure if they lived near us. The first order of the day was to buy furniture for all of those new rooms. My lovely angel had been right about saving money for furniture. Luckily, we had saved enough money for furniture and accessories. Summer was soon over and Rose started planning for Christmas in our new home. That was fine with me but I told her there were a few things I needed to do to the house first.

We both agreed to get the house in tiptop shape and wait until the next year to celebrate Christmas in our new home. Before moving into our house, we went to see mama. This time she seemed much better. In fact, she was happier than ever. She held her grandchildren and spoke lovingly to them. None of the kids knew Italian, but that didn't matter to them. Her words had a melodic sound to them as they listened and smiled the smiles of love. This is the way it should have always been for mama, she should have been experiencing the serenity and calm of sharing love. After our visit, I again questioned the doctor about the possibility of mama visiting her family once in a while. I knew the answer before I even asked the question, but I just couldn't pass it up.

The doctor restated the many reasons why that could never happen, so I left there disappointed as ever.

We moved into our new home in November as planned. Every night and every weekend I worked on the house. With the connections I had in the construction business, I was able to raise a dormer that fitted two bedrooms, a full bath, kitchen, and living room. Rose thought I was overdoing it. "Why do we need so many rooms?" she asked.

"Rose, we may need the extra rooms someday for our family."

"Joe, do you plan to keep our daughters under our roof forever?"

I replied, "Maybe. At least that is my reasoning. I don't know. I just want our little home expanded for any possibility." I thought to myself, "If my lady is questioning my first venture, what will she think about the rest of my plans for reconstruction?"

By the beginning of 1949, I was half way finished with converting the basement into a recreation room. I already had the wet bar, bathroom, and laundry room in working condition. This work really pleased Rose and the girls.

Rose knew that having the family over was going to be very comfortable for all, and the girls had a place to play during the winter. When I told Rose that I also wanted to add a porch to the front of the house, and a porch from the kitchen to the back yard she laughed and said, "When does the pool go in?"

I thought to myself, "You never can tell, angel. Maybe sooner than you think." I was already making plans for a summer of leisure for my girls. That, though, will be my anniversary gift to Rose. I thought, "Maybe not this year but definitely by next summer."

When July came around, I was exhausted. We hadn't made any vacation plans so we thought we'd go to Coney Island on the weekends and figure out some other recreational things for the girls to do. Our summer plans hit an all time high when we received a call from Gene. He and his family were coming to New York for a few weeks. I called Rose in to hear our conversation. I told Gene that I knew just right the place for them to spend their vacation. Rose started jumping up and down shouting, "Stay here." What a great way this would be to celebrate our first summer in our new home. The attic would accommodate his family very comfortably.

Gene and Inez loved our attic apartment and we spent every waking hour together. We had two great state parks in our area for picnicking and row boating. They were the Valley Stream State Park and the Hecksher State Park. Mama Anna and Rose's three youngest sisters spent a weekend with us too, and we all went picnicking. We had a houseful, and Rose and the girls were delighted. While Gene was with us, the rest of the family dropped in and also brought all kinds of good news with them. My brothers Angelo and Mike had bought houses near us also.

Rose's brother Paul was looking for a house in our area, too. Rose was just beaming with all the good news especially when she heard that Mary and Sal were expecting their first baby in January. Our combined families meant everything to us. I just wished that Gene could visit more often. We missed him.

Summer ended too quickly. We were content. Doreen was becoming a lovely young lady and Eileen was glued to her big sister's hip. Doreen had been skipped in school a couple of times and would be starting the ninth grade in September. She was nervous about going to high school with the kids being so much older than she, but it all worked out just fine. Eileen missed Doreen during school hours so Rose and her new friend in the neighborhood, Connie, would get together every day with their two daughters for a playtime and coffee klatch. Apparently, Rose had been talking to Connie about missing her job at the book bindery because she told me one night that Connie had offered to babysit Eileen if Rose wanted to go back to work. I wasn't happy about her traveling to work by bus and train, but if she really felt that was something she had to do, then I could never say no to her. So Rose went back to work. I never thought she'd want to go back once we had a house and two daughters. I was kind of disappointed. This wasn't the way it was supposed to be. A wife and mother stayed home with her family.

Well times they were a changing and my angel was never behind the times. That was just one of the reasons why I adored her.

Chapter 59

It was one week before Christmas when Sam called with shocking news. He had heard from our Aunt Jeanette again. This time, she had what she considered good news for us. She had been in Italy and France for the past few years and, lo and behold guess who she found?

I could tell Sam was busting to tell all, but he was having a grand old time dragging it out. During the war, our mama's family fled Italy and Mussolini's fascist regime seeking safety in France. Aunt Jeanette was able to track them down and, after a lot of red tape, she was able to bring two people back with her. I could care less. All I could think of was how amazing it was that she could track down family on another continent but couldn't find her sister and her sister's sons in America so many years ago? One of the people she brought back with her was the youngest daughter, Marie, of another one of mama's sisters. I couldn't stop myself from being so resentful of our "aunt" so I just spit out "Oh, how caring of her towards her newfound niece. What other cousin did she bring back?"

Sam said, "Brace yourself. She didn't bring back another one of her family members, she brought papa home."

Brace myself? Was Sam kidding? My emotions were going haywire. Do I care? Do I not care? Sam said, "Papa is in Connecticut with Aunt Jeanette and would like to see us."

"What?" I screamed "He would like to see us... now? Look, if you want to see him, go right ahead. It's almost time to visit mama and she comes way before a visit to see him." Sam said he'd go see papa and tell us all about the old man on our way to see mama.

I said, "So be it. Just make sure you make it back to New York in time or we'll have to go without you." I knew I was being rough on Sam. I was ashamed of my behavior, but this news was just too harrowing for me.

Sam made it back in plenty of time and told us about papa on our way to see mama. He said papa was a little man, about 5 feet, 5 inches tall, spoke very little English, and was shabbily dressed. The two of them talked about papa's return to Sicily and how he had escaped to France.

Eventually, papa met up with Mama's family. He tried to get back to America, but between the war and the poverty he could not come home to mama and us. Since returning to America a few months prior he found work on an apple orchard. He wanted to see mama and all of his sons as soon as possible, because his health was failing and he wanted to make peace with his family.

So that was it then. Papa's back and wants a family reunion. God forgive me, but I had become a doubting Thomas with mixed feelings of love and hate. Angelo and Mike were very mixed on their feelings too. After much deliberation, we decided the only thing to do was to go and see him in the spring. I finished my home renovations in April and the four of us headed for Connecticut.

Chapter 60

When we arrived at Aunt Jeanette's house, she led us out to her backyard where papa was waiting for us. One look at him and the ice in my veins melted. He was not the papa I remembered. As Sam had said, he was small in stature, dressed in an old, white shirt, and black trousers that looked ready for the garbage can. If I'd passed him on the street, I would have given him a handout; he looked that poor.

I was actually happy to see him. His smile was infectious. His eyes had a spark of mischievousness in them. And though he was small in stature, he carried himself like a giant. When he spoke, his voice had a musical lilt to it. This man was no pauper; he had a wealth of spirit, humor, charm, and a zest for life. I asked how he was physically since he looked so robust. He said he felt fine, and that the doctors didn't know what they had been talking about. When I asked him what the doctors thought was wrong with him, he patted his chest, smiled, and tilted his head as if to say what do they know?

Sam wanted to know what papa's arrangement was with Aunt Jeanette. Did he have to stay in Connecticut? Papa said he wanted to see mama and all of his sons in New York. I told papa he could come back with us, and that I knew the perfect place where he could live. I swear if I were Irish, I'd say he looked just like a little leprechaun about to do an Irish jig. I called Rose and told her how our meeting with papa had gone.

The first words out of her mouth were "Bring him home Joe. He belongs here with you and we have just the place for him." My angel came through again. Rose, Doreen, and Eileen fell in love with him at first sight.

Here it was 1950 and I was with my papa once again after twenty-three years. I never realized how much I'd missed him until he was finally back with us. We loved his company and the stories he told us of his wanderings in Italy and France, and of his longing to be here with us in America. The war had left his homeland in need of much repair, and there were so many people left homeless and starving. When the United States Army finally ousted the Germans he began to look for ways to get back to America, but he had never become a U.S. citizen, and it looked hopeless until Aunt Jeanette arrived in France. He begged for her help and she was able to get him home. Now he had but one final wish. He must see his beautiful wife Grace once again and the rest of his sons.

Tony and Phil made it home in July so the only one missing was Lou. Without further delay we six sons and papa went to see mama. Papa was smoking his cheroot and humming to himself. He looked genuinely happy. When we got to the hospital, we left papa in the hall while we went in to see mama. We told her that we'd forgotten something and had to leave for a minute. As we walked out papa walked in. The last thing we saw as we closed the door was mama in the arms of her husband once again.

Half an hour later, he was still in the room with her. We didn't want to get in their way, but we knew the strain of the day would soon get to her. As we went back into the room, we saw papa combing and braiding mama's hair. They were both humming a song from their past. Mama looked at us and said, "My Mikey still loves me."

Papa leaned over and while kissing her ear said, "Mikey will love you forever." That moment and those words were what we had all longed to hear all of our lives.

Chapter 61

Mama and papa were together again and happy once more. But sometimes happiness is cut short. As mama was kissing all of us goodbye, she fell asleep. Papa fell on his knees and begged for her forgiveness. But it was too late; his words had fallen on deaf ears.

The next four months were spent loving and caring for papa. He had been steadily losing weight and becoming more and more listless. We cancelled our summer vacation plans because papa was too weak to travel and we didn't want to leave him alone. When papa first came to live with us, he walked around the neighborhood and made friends with everybody. He planted an apple tree on the front lawn and cared for it day after day. He loved the feel and fragrance of the earth. While holding the soil in his hand he said, "This is God's gift to us, and we must always take care of it because it cradles the souls of the departed."

As it was getting closer to Christmas, he spent most of his time sitting in the rocking chair on the front porch. When I complained that it was too cold outside for him, he would just shrug his shoulders and say, "Life is cold." I loved my papa once again. I would sometimes wish that we could turn back time and correct the path that we had all taken. Whatever papa had done was in the past. I could not resent him any longer. He

159

had paid his dues and just wanted to be with his family at the end.

I finally got him to go with me to the doctor. He said he knew it was a waste of time because he knew his body, and he could tell the doctor what was wrong with him. He was only fifty-nine. I was sure he was just ill from his long journey back to us. But, he was right. When the doctor told him he was very ill, Papa said, "I know. It's the Big C isn't it?" The doctor told him that there was nothing that could be done at that late stage of the illness. If we wanted our papa to live the rest of his life surrounded by those who loved him, it would be better for him not to be hospitalized. He gave papa a chance to consider what he wanted to do and papa said, "Joey, can we just go home now? I want to see mama."

He never did get another chance to see mama. One week later, on an exceptionally beautiful autumn day, he fell asleep in his rocking chair and left us forever. Fortunately, he had left after finding love again. His love for his wife and sons had come back to him. He did love us after all. And we still loved him. My biggest regrets were that he hadn't seen mama one more time, and that we didn't have more time with him. All I could think was that he made it home in time. We were all given a second chance to reunite with the father we had missed for too many years. I will never forget the love we shared for each other while he was in my home.

I have heard it said that people in mourning tend to believe that their departed loved one is still very near them. Well, a strange thing occurred on the day we set papa to rest. The night was starless and overcast as Rose, Doreen, Eileen, and I were driving home from the cemetery. It was a long, slow ride on the parkway, and Rose fell asleep with Eileen in her arms. Doreen was in the back seat with her head against the window, she was very quiet and probably missing grandpa very much already.

It was pretty late and we seemed to be the only car on the road that night. There was no mist on the road, and my car windows were all clear. About five car lengths ahead of me I thought I saw a hitchhiker on the side of the road. I slowed down a bit and gasped at what I saw. Rose jumped awake and asked why I had moaned. I told her I thought I saw someone hitching a ride. Before I could say anything else Doreen said "Daddy why didn't you stop for grandpa?"

I think, perhaps, papa was given a chance to say goodbye to us after all. I never told a soul about that night, or what Doreen and I thought we saw. Doreen and Rose never mentioned it again and neither did I. Whatever we saw it was not frightening, but in a comforting way, it gave us an insight to what could be waiting for all of us...a new life after death. No one knows what becomes of our souls when we die. We have all been taught through all religions that life, as we know it doesn't end when we leave this earth. I will be the first to admit that if it be possible, I will find a way to always be with my three angels even after I'm gone.

Chapter 62

Lou, Tony, and Phil were all home in time for our visit to mama. We agreed not to mention anything about papa's demise to her; we would just say that he had to work. Thankfully, she had no conception of one day from another, so we could get away with a lie like that. When we arrived, we took turns sitting with her so that a crowd wouldn't be too much for her. For some unknown reason, she looked radiant that day. She was well groomed and smiled continuously. She held the children and snuggled them. It turned out to be one of the best days we had ever had with mama. We were all pretty depressed over papa's passing but she brightened up the day for us.

She had picked up quite a bit of English over the past few years, and could hold a good conversation with anybody, even in her broken-English way. Near the end of our visit she asked everybody if she could have a few moments alone with her sons. This was so totally unlike her, but everyone agreed and left the room except for we seven brothers.

When we were alone with mama she beckoned us, one at a time, to come to her. As we did as she requested, she first gave each of us a crushing hug and then four kisses. One kiss on our forehead, one kiss on each cheek, and the last kiss on our lips. She had made the sign of the cross with her kisses and when she was finished she made the sign of the cross on herself and said a prayer in Italian. When this rite, or whatever it was, was

162

over she said, "May the Spirit of Christ always be in your hearts. My Mikey has gone to be with God. When it is my time, I will be with him again, and when it is your time, you will be with papa and mama forever." We just looked at her, speechless. She added, "Now, go home to your beautiful families and live long, happy lives with loving memories of your papa." And that was that. What a day to remember. Mama was back.

The ride home was the same for all of us. We couldn't speak of what had happened while only the seven of us were with mama. That would have to wait till we had a quiet moment alone with our wives. Tony and Phil came home with us since they had given up their apartments when they went into the Army. They would be out of the Army soon anyway so we told them they could have our upstairs apartment for as long as they wanted. Phil and Doreen became great friends and he assumed the position of guardian to her. She didn't object to that at all because all of her friends became his friends and she felt safe with his attention and caring.

Despite the sorrow of losing papa, Christmas was a comforting celebration of love regained and family unity. The year 1950 had been one of learning and gratitude for me. I learned how to forgive and forget past transgressions and how to be grateful for the short period of time I'd been given with papa. I will never forget the love he brought to all of us. For the first time in many years we were able to see mama express a wisdom we had never seen before and a happiness for the love she hadn't shared for a very long time. Seeing mama and papa reunited and still deeply in love lifted our hearts and cast away the pains of the past. It had been a good year in many ways.

Chapter 63

Eileen was growing so fast and with her blond hair and blue, eyes she was a beautiful standout among other children. Rose was content with her job, and I finished our home renovations with an in-ground swimming pool that turned our home into a summer retreat for the whole family. The year 1951 was starting out pretty good too. Spring and summer had zoomed by thanks to all the good family activity we were all enjoying in our home. And before we knew it, the end of the year holidays were not far off. I thought, "Why must another year of happiness end in sorrow?"

One week before Thanksgiving, the hospital called to say that Mama was having health problems. We all rushed to the hospital but it was too late. Almost exactly one year after papa's death, mama joined him. She had just turned fifty-nine. We never had a chance to say goodbye to her either. The doctor said it was as though she had willed herself to take the long sleep. She had the usual problems, but nothing to foresee a serious condition. On the evening of her passing, she had been very happy and lucid. She told the evening nurse to tell her sons how much she had always loved them.

Her exact words were, "I have loved them all my life and I will love them forever. Mikey needs me now and I need him." The next morning they found her still in bed with a smile on her lips. She had passed over peacefully. As distraught as I

164

was, I couldn't help but feel relief for mama. She was finally at a happy place, and I was sure papa was with her.

Looking back on my family's history reminded me that Rose's family had suffered throughout their lifetime as well. Mama Anna's life had not been an easy one either. With all the memories she'd told about her life in Sicily, there was one she kept secret for almost forty years. Lena and Flo had found some old letters and photos, that mama Anna had hidden away. The girls had been cleaning house and came upon them quite by accident. When they asked Mama Anna about the items they'd found, she said it didn't concern them and she hurriedly hid them away again. Flo was distressed and told Anna, who told Mary, who told Rose, who told Jenny who decided to keep the brothers out of it. Jenny went to mama and told her that everything in mama's life was important to her family, so mama called the girls together for a meeting. Of course, Rose told me there was to be a meeting and made me swear never to repeat what mama was about to tell them. Until this moment, I have always kept mama's secret to myself. When all of her daughters were seated, she told them the following:

At the age of fourteen, she married a young man from her village. One year later they had a son. He was a beautiful boy but very sickly. Six months later a terrible illness spread through their village. Many people died from this illness, and among them were her husband, her little brother, and her father. Her son was spared but he remained a sickly child.

A little over a year later a handsome young man named Bartelomeo, came to her village to visit his relatives. Her late husband had been his cousin, so he came to her house to see how she and his cousin's son were faring. They had never met before, but they were both immediately smitten with each other. Her year of mourning had long passed so she agreed to be courted by him. After a couple of months, he told her that he had made plans to leave for America before meeting her, and the time for leaving was drawing near. She was devastated. He begged her to marry him and go to America with him. Although she loved him deeply, she told him that she would

165

not go with him because her son was too ill to travel such a long distance. Their love for each other would have to remain unfulfilled, and they must never see each other again. He was so saddened by her rejection that he left the village to go back to his family.

Mama missed him with all her heart and became very depressed at her loss. She had no way of knowing that Bartelomeo was also depressed being away from her. Mama's mother said to her "Either get him out of your heart or go with him." But no, mama could never take the chance that her son might not live because of the stress of such a long journey. Her mother told her " If you truly love this man, you should go to America with him, and I will send your son to you as soon as he is strong enough to travel." But no this was too impossible for her to do. Her mother said, "You would not leave your son for a short time with his grandmother who loves him as much as the son she herself has lost?" While mother and daughter were arguing, there was a knock at the door. Bartelomeo had come back to her. He pleaded with her to marry him and said that he was willing to give up his trip to America and stay there with her and her son.

Mama Anna was so thrilled, that she said yes immediately. They started making plans for their wedding, when she suddenly realized that he was giving up his dream for her. She could not do that to the man she loved, and called off the wedding. She broke his heart again, but she could not deprive him of the life he could have without her. Her mother couldn't take the torment between them any longer and told her to just go and be happy. She promised that little Cosmo would be well taken care of, and that he would be sent to them as soon as he was better and they could afford his transportation. So they were married and left for America. Mama Anna yearned for her son Cosmo and longed for the day she could hold him in her arms again. But that day never came. She hadn't seen her baby boy for some forty years. She never gave up hope though. She still prayed for the day when they would finally be reunited. She had been keeping the pictures and letters that were sent to her throughout his years of growing up. One of the letters told that he was he was married with twin sons, and they longed to see mama Anna, too.

Wow! How she kept such a secret all those years was amazing. But why was it a secret? She told her daughters "My shame was never meant to be told. I committed a grave sin when I left my baby son behind. He never had the chance to be with his mother and sisters and brothers. I was selfish. I felt the anguish of his not being safe with me in America. How many times I have dreamed of the agony he must have been going through during the years of the war. I was being punished by not knowing if he was alive or dead. I will be forever punished." No, no. All this from the woman who has been the most loving and caring of any woman I knew. I wished I could tell her how wonderful a mother she had been; not only to her own children, but to all of us she took under her wing, and shared her motherly love with. That time in her life had not proved her selfish. The son she felt she wronged, would always love her because he shares the same beautiful, heartwarming soul she has.

Chapter 64

The fifties were adding to all the changes that even my generation has seen. If we go back only one hundred years, it's amazing how advanced a civilization we've become, and the prospects for so many more achievements is mind-boggling. I'm one of those guys that like to tell the kids, "In my time..." The kids might laugh, but if only they could really see how different life was only twenty, thirty or forty years ago. If only they could get pulled by a trolley car while on their roller skates. Or feel the excitement of sitting around a family radio listening to a spooky story, and using their imaginations to picture what a monster might look like. But why bother with radios when you could go to a drive-in movie complex to see all the monsters and love stories right there on the silver screen while in your car?

Of course, the threat of an atomic bomb falling out of the sky loomed over the whole country. Even I was contemplating building a bomb shelter for my family. No wonder the kids today were trying to get their lives in hurry-up mode. The new music, rock and roll, was driving them to a frenzy of wild, hip swinging, and too-sexy dancing. Sure the 1920s were wild, and maybe I'm just getting too old in my ways to see any correlation between those years and the '50s. Their feelings seem to be, live it all today because tomorrow may never come. As if the A Bomb wasn't enough, President Truman had ordered the construction of another deadly weapon, the H Bomb.

God help us if we ever have another war. Our family was content to just keeping moving along and we were still growing. Little sisters Anna and Flo were women now.

Anna met and married a young sailor named Bill, and they got an apartment near mama Anna. We took mama on a lot of vacation trips with us, but could never convince her to move in with us. Little Florence was engaged to a nice guy, Pat, and Lena made her choice to never get married, and to stay with mama always. Mama Anna didn't have to worry about ever being lonely. Her daughters made sure that at least one of them would stop in for a visit every day. She was well loved by her whole family.

Our lives, Rose, Doreen, Eileen, and me, were better than ever. And then one day everything changed. We had the most unbelievable surprise from right out of the blue.

The year was 1953 and we were living the good life. We had a beautiful house with all the amenities, money in the bank, great vacations, a terrific relationship with our extended families, two gorgeous daughters, and didn't think we could ask for anything more. That was until the miracle of miracles happened to us. We were pregnant again. It was so incredibly unexpected and unplanned. What a Christmas gift this turned out to be. Happy New Year 1954, we were to be greeting our new child in September.

That pregnancy was a good one for Rose, too. Without any complications, she delivered our third daughter, Marie, on September 28. We named her Marie because she was a gift from the Blessed Mother, and we jokingly said that she was an immaculate conception. When I saw Marie for the first time, I couldn't get over how much she resembled me. She had bright, red hair, hazel or blue eyes (it was too soon to tell yet), skin like a porcelain doll, and a set of lungs that bespoke of a future in entertainment. Just like her old dad. I felt like the luckiest man on earth. I had another sweet angel to love.

Doreen had graduated from high school in June and was working as a legal secretary at a law firm in Hempstead. She had turned down my offer to have Hermes Pan as her master dance teacher, and as for college, she didn't want that either. She complained that college for women was only if they wanted to become teachers or nurses and find a rich guy to marry. Her dancing would continue but not at Carnegie Hall. She didn't think her dancing skills were good enough yet. She was sweet sixteen and had a mind of her own. Whatever she wanted, I would be there for her.

Now Eileen on the other hand, was already seven years old and in the third grade. I was really worried about her. Doreen would not be with her as usual and a new baby might make her suddenly feel left out. She really never had Rose completely with her since she was two. Doreen was more like a mother to her than a sister. Rose had never neglected her daughters. She loved them with all her heart, and made sure they knew how much she loved them every night after work and on the weekends. I know children expect more from their mothers, and accept that their fathers aren't available all the time, but Rose truly enjoyed working. It gave her a feeling of accomplishment. Well it was much to my surprise and that of our girls, that when Rose and Marie came home from the hospital she declared to all of us that she would not be working any longer. She was going to be a stay-at-home mother from that day on. Life couldn't be any better for my angels.

Chapter 65

The year 1954 ran right into 1960. When had everything zoomed ahead like that? We survived the 1950s and the 1960s looked better and better every day. Science had moved on in leaps and bounds. Dr. Salk found a cure for Polio, jet planes flew the skies, and televisions had color instead of just black and white. TV shows took on a life of their own. Americans were now gathering around their TV set to see stars like Eddy Cantor.

There was Ed Sullivan and his Show of Shows, "Uncle Milty" (Milton Berle) and the kids even had shows of their own to watch. There was Howdy Doody, Superman, Kukla, Fran and Ollie, Roy Rogers, and Dick Clark's *American Bandstand.* Children's toys were even becoming fads. The Hula Hoop, Mr. Potato Head, Silly Putty, and the Slinky were all favorites. And best of all, the Korean War had ended.

Time was racing by for our family too. Rose kept to her word and never went back to work. In 1955, Doreen married Bill, a Navy veteran of the Korean War and they had three sons, Billy, Joey, and Timmy. They bought a house out in Suffolk County, but we still got to see them quite often, even though it was almost an hour drive away. I missed her very much and Rose missed her little "Twinkle Toes" too. She was happy, we were happy for her and Eileen missed her a lot. Marie loved her little nephews, who were only slightly younger than herself, and I think she loved the fact that she was "older" than them and could boss them around.

My little girl had the sons I never had. I was so thrilled with my daughters that I had never even considered what having sons would have been like. They were great little guys but totally different from the soft, quiet girls I'd helped raise. Being a grandfather was a whole new ball game for me. I couldn't get over that. Rose and I were not old fogies yet, but we were bona fide grandparents and loving it. When did our little girl become a woman? I couldn't remember. I took a long, hard look at Eileen and a chill ran up my spine. She was already thirteen and beautiful. How many years did we have left before she was to become a full-fledged woman and leave us for some guy? And then was Marie. Would she be out of our home in another fifteen years or so? Time had to slow up a little. I thought, "Thank God Rose and I will always have each other." life was good though and we were all happy. But as usual just when everything seemed perfect, something always happened to break our hearts. Mama Anna was no longer with us. Her passing was the end of decades of love and joy that she had bestowed on all of us. It was so unexpected. Only a year before, she had her gall bladder removed and went through the surgery with flying colors. Apparently she wasn't as recuperated as she had led us all to believe. She never complained and seemed to be all better. The aftermath of the surgery had taken its toll on her. Mama Anna forged the bond that kept the family all together. I thought, "God bless you Mama, you must surely have a seat at the right hand of God." Once again we were a family mourning for the loss of our most dearest.

Chapter 66

Our united families were changing too. On Rose's side, Gene had retired and he, Inez and their baby son, Kenny, moved to California. Their son Bart was married and living in California too. Doris, their first born, was a nun stationed in Guatamala. Mary and Sal and Paul and Louise bought their new homes near Doreen. Mary and Sal had two daughters and two sons, Frankie, Bart, JoAnne, and AnnaMarie. Paul and Louise also had two sons and two daughters, Josephine, Janet, Paul, and Bruce. Anna and Bill had two daughters, LuAnne and Diane, and Flo and Pat had a daughter named Gina and a son named Pat. Lena had chosen to live alone.

Our families had grown and prospered, and we were still united. Mama Anna had a lot to do with that. I just hoped that we could still keep it together. They say absence makes the heart grow fonder. Our love for mama Anna would never lessen to the point where it might need reinforcing. I thought, "I'll see you in my dreams mama Anna."

My brothers and I, who had a very short family life as kids, had all, well almost all of us, become husbands and fathers despite our pasts. Sam and Vinnie were living in Queens with their son Bobby and daughter Theresa. Mike and Millie lived near us with their daughters Delores and Loretta. Angelo and Anne also lived near us with their only son Larry. Lou retired from the Navy and was living the life of a bachelor in California.

Tony married our cousin from France, Marie, and they had two daughters named Michelle and Joanne. They lived in Brooklyn. Phil married Terri, who lived near us too, and had two sons named Joseph and Michael. It seemed like a miracle that seven, almost forgotten kids, made a life for themselves filled with love and happiness after all. I was thinking about how you never can tell what heights you can climb to once you've found the love of a woman. "Thank you Rose my angel."

The rest of the sixties were filled with great changes and a lot of sorrow. Those were the years that will be remembered in the annals of the history of the United States. Hawaii became our fiftieth state. The Civil Rights Movement was on the march with leaders like Malcolm X and Martin Luther King, Jr. Some Americans were protesting our entry into the Vietnam War, and women were burning their bras in their fight for Women's Liberation. Fidel Castro had taken over the leadership of Cuba and all American properties in that country. The people of Cuba were fleeing Castro for sanctuary in Florida. President Eisenhower was succeeded for the presidency by Senator John F. Kennedy, a young man with great ideas. President Kennedy began our space program, which had been jump-started by Russia with their first orbit around the earth. He initiated the Peace Corps, pushed for better science and math education, and proposed tax cuts. He was also a believer in the benefits of the arts and entertainment.

The Civil Rights Movement, feminism, and gay rights were pushing full steam ahead. There were riots, sit-ins, protests, and marches by people from all walks of life. The one thing that really bothered me were the rebellious young people who believed in open sex and taking drugs. I believed they were the ones who referred to those times as "The Swinging Sixties" where anything goes, because of the libertine attitudes that were being thrown around. This really worried me because I still had two young, impressionable daughters at home. The last thing Rose and I needed was for them to get into that way of life. What were we coming to, another Sodom and Gomorrah? God forbid.

Chapter 67

And then disaster struck. On November 22, 1963, our country was horribly sent into mourning by one very sick man. The whole world rocked and the United States reeled in shock and despair on this day that will never be forgotten. Our most beloved president ever, John F. Kennedy, was assassinated in Dallas, Texas. Television caught the horror on video, and police captured the alleged assassin Harvey Oswald, who was murdered by Jack Ruby, while in custody. As if the tragedy of losing our president wasn't bad enough, the TV stations showed it over and over again adding to the misery we were already feeling. The world mourned the death of our president. He will never be forgotten.

The year 1963 ended with a sadness in America and a new president, L.B. Johnson. Our family continued to grow and prosper. We were all doing well in 1964 and sorely missed our Christmas trips to mama, which were only fading memories now. So far so good. The following year, 1965, seemed to have started well until February. Losing a loved one is devastating. But what of the loved ones who were left behind? How does one cope?

In February of 1965, Doreen's husband Bill died after having heart surgery. His death was devastating to his wife and three little sons. In a conflicting way, this was like the Kennedy assassination, except this was our family. A young widow, our daughter, and three, very young, fatherless sons, ages eight, seven, and four, our grandsons, had to endure an extremely sorrowful military funeral. Their future was in the hands of God with a lot of help from all of all us who loved them.

The year 1965 came to its end with another assassination, it was the sudden demise of Civil Rights activist, Malcolm X.

The year 1966 had become a year of coping and overcoming for Doreen and her boys. They were thriving and growing despite their loneliness. Our little beauty Eileen was happily married to her childhood sweetheart Denis, and although she was out of our home, she and Denis lived close enough for regular family visits. It was finally a good year for Doreen in 1967. She met and married Al. The remarkable thing was that Doreen had found love again, and her young man not only loved her, but wanted to adopt her sons. Doreen felt it was best for her sons to keep their fathers name so she said no to the idea of adoption. Right after the wedding, they all moved to California to start a new life together.

And so the 1960s were drawing near to an end when disaster struck again. In 1968, there were two more assassinations. What the hell was going on in America? Politicians and do-gooders were being killed left and right. The most honored Civil Rights pursuer, Martin Luther King, Jr., was shot and killed in April. But the hatred didn't stop there. In June, Robert F. Kennedy, the brother and Attorney General of our late President John F. Kennedy, was killed during his campaign for the presidency.

The Kennedy family and the world would never forget the sorrow bestowed upon that great family in the 1960s.

By the end of 1969 we had elected Richard Nixon to be our president. Oh well, one can never tell. Maybe he would make himself worthy of his new title. Meanwhile, a new culture called hippies were running around half naked and protesting everything they could think of, if they could even think straight with all the drugs they were consuming. These changes and occurrences were mind boggling to me. I thought,

"If we make it to 1970, will we be able to show the world that we are still a strong nation? Only time will tell."

Rose and I were now in our fifties, and she still looked as vibrant and beautiful as ever. The only change in our life together was the further deepening of our love for one another and our family.

Chapter 68

The 1970s started out great, and as usual held many changes for our family. Doreen and Al retuned to New York and bought a house in Suffolk County. They needed a big house because they had blessed our family with two more grandchildren. Our first granddaughter, Deirdre, and our fifth grandson, Brett. Eileen and Denis had introduced grandson number four, Denis Michael, and grandson number six, Brian, to our ever-growing family. So we now had six grandsons and one granddaughter. Doreen's children had a head start on our other grandchildren, and her two eldest sons, Billy and Joey, would be getting married by 1977. But before that was to happen, Marie married her childhood boyfriend Joe and what do you know? Two more grandsons, Joseph and Nicholas. I couldn't be prouder of my daughters. They had given me what I had never been able to provide for my angel Rose and myself, which was a family full of males again.

Eight grandsons and one adorable little granddaughter. I walked around with the biggest inflated chest ever. Our family's future would be in their hands one day and I knew in my heart that they would continue to make our family grow and prosper. Thank goodness our little Deirdre would continue to carry on the beauty of their grandmother. She was already a spitting image of Doreen who was an uncanny duplicate of Rose.

My only regret with having so many grandsons was the thought of what the future could have in store for them. Not that life might not be hard for my little granddaughter too, but at least she wouldn't have to go off to war. I thought, maybe, God willing, the world would be a better place to be in by the time they all reach adulthood. As for my angel Rose, all the happiness we had shared so far couldn't hold a candle to the love and happiness she felt for our grandkids. I had given her everything I promised those many years ago and now her daughters had added to her bliss.

Marie and Joe had moved in with us for a little while, and that sure made things easier when I had to go to Kentucky to get another project started. I hated leaving Rose but I was grateful that she wasn't alone. When all of our girls were married, the house had become too quiet and lonely. Thankfully, they had all taken turns living with us for a short while before their houses were ready to be moved into. I couldn't imagine how we'd feel with just the two of us again.

Chapter 69

God help me, but my world was changing again, and not for the good either. Rose and I were so happy and content with our family and each other, when I was hit with another crushing blow to my soul. My brother, my big, father-like brother Sam died. Just two weeks before his daughter's wedding he died of a heart attack. He was only fifty-nine.

The age that seemed to curse my family. It was so sudden. No warning. One minute he was happy and bowling with friends, and the next he was gone. He was gone forever from my life and his wife and children. Sam and I shared so much for so many years, but that could never be again. It was too soon and he was too young. If it wasn't for Rose and our family, I could not have gone on without him. We talked Theresa into going ahead with the wedding because Sam wouldn't have wanted it any other way. And Sam was there that day, in all of our hearts and thoughts.

I thought to myself, "Goodbye brother. I know that you are finally with mama and papa, as it always should have been when we were children. I will miss you always. You were a big part of my life from the day I was born until the day you left this earth. I'll see you in my dreams." And I did.

Sleep had become impossible for me. I was afraid to go to sleep because of the nightmares that had started when Sam died. I felt like death was looming over me. My dreams always started and ended the same way, Sam, mama, and papa were calling for me, and Rose would end my dream by pulling my arm away from them and Sam pulling my other arm towards them. I was being torn apart. When I would finally awaken it was always 2:00 a.m. I began to speculate that the meaning of my dream was my certain death at 2:00 a.m. on the day of my fifty-ninth birthday. This was my night terror and I could not share it with my beloved Rose.

During one of Doreen's visits, I overheard the conversation she and Rose were having about me. My sweet Rose was worried over my sleepless nights and obvious nightmares. She would see me tossing and turning and so overly restless in my sleep. Rose said that when I cried out in my sleep, without waking me she would pull down my outstretched arm and cuddle up to me. She was afraid to tell me what I'd been doing every night. My God, what a woman. She was my angel after all. She kept me safe and comforted even in my sleep.

I waited until we were alone that night and told Rose all about my nightmares. She then confessed to me that she had been aware of them too. I told Rose that "Once more you've been my shining light and I regret that I haven't done the same for you." She threw her arms around me and said "Mr. Bones, you have given me everything any woman could have ever wished for. These dreams are only reflecting your fears. You will be around for a long time to come because I could never live without you." As usual my angel was right. My fifty-ninth birthday came and went and I was still around.

To make things even better, my grandson Billy became engaged to his bride to be MaryRose and they set the date for October 1977. One month later, his brother Joey and his girlfriend Agnes announced their engagement, and set their wedding date for August 1977. Well it looked like the '70s would be good in many ways after all. There would be more good memories for Rose and me to share.

Chapter 70

I began reminiscing of my years past as maitre de and manager of entertainment of the club I'd been working in for so many years. One of my projects was a Wednesday night amateur talent show. A few of our winners had become celebrities and never forgot where they got their start at entertaining in front of an audience. One year Rose and I had taken a trip to Las Vegas to see one of the winning kids who had made the big time.

He had become a very popular comedian and was now starring in his own show in Las Vegas. I was floored when he announced my presence to the audience and presented a silver bullet, his signature, on a necklace to my Rose. He turned out to be a great guy who never forgot his roots. Several other winners made it big too. Another comedian turned to acting, and it felt strange seeing him in a non-comedic role as a Mafioso. His brother, who also was one of our winners, sang his way to success as did a young woman with a voice like Billie Holiday. I was proud of all of them and happy to have been there for their show biz beginnings. Yep the '70s had been great so far. But the '70s weren't over yet and my life was about to become a living hell.

Chapter 71

In the spring when Rose started her pre-summer cleaning, I decided it was about time I gave her a hand with it. I didn't like her doing it all by herself now that the girls were all busy doing there own homes. I took some time off from work and was really getting into the cleaning bit. What surprised me was that Rose never complained about my efforts. Since I'd never done it before I thought she'd be following me around with a white glove. Well, it was a good feeling anyway. I was feeling quite proud of myself. I thought to myself, "Who loves you, baby? Ain't I great?" Rose just shrugged her shoulders and smiled. When all the spring cleaning was finished, inside and outside, we were ready to bask in the summer sun and enjoy our family.

Maybe it was just me, but I felt Rose was not as happy as I was. She was kind of out of it. I said, "Hey, angel. Is everything all right? Did I mess something up? I can fix it if you tell me what is wrong."

"Oh Joe. It's just these darn headaches. I can't get rid of them."

"Rosie, maybe it's the new eyeglasses. The prescription could be too strong."

Rose refused to go back to the eye doctor. She wanted to wait until after the weddings. Of course my brave lady wanted

186

to wait. She always thought of everybody else's needs before those of her own. Well, I thought if I couldn't convince her to go for a checkup, maybe our daughters could.

All three of my girls had noticed changes in their mother lately. For some time, each one had seen her trip or lose her balance and naturally Rose blamed it on her eyeglasses, or anything that might have been in her way. When we all started putting one thing after another together, a chill ran up my spine. Something was definitely wrong and my lady needed help right away. We all herded Rose to the eye doctor against her wishes. God forgive me for being so blind. I was the one who should have picked up on it right away. What had I done?

After a thorough examination, the doctor told me to get Rose to the hospital E.R. immediately. He was certain that she had been having minor strokes and needed medical attention right away. With the strength and courage Rose had been endowed with, she insisted the doctor didn't know what he was talking about, but to make us happy she would go to the hospital. She was ready to tell us "I told you so. Now, who will be the first to apologize?" The next few hours in the hospital were torture for us. Rose was a trooper. She submitted to every test and all the poking and probing with a look of, "Wait till I get you home." But home for Rose was not to be in the very near future.

The next test the doctor was preparing to do was an angiogram. He advised us to go home but I said no. There was no way I, or the girls, would be leaving my angel alone.

After the girls hugged and kissed her, they went to sit in the waiting room. I couldn't walk away from my angel. I wanted to be with her wherever they took her. She suddenly looked so frail, and I saw a faint trace of fear in her eyes. I wrapped my arms around her.

When it was time for her to go for the angiogram she held me close to her heart and told me not to be afraid. Imagine my sweet angel was comforting me? At a time like that I should be the one doing the comforting, but I was too frightened and struggling to keep my tears from flowing. I thought, "Oh my love, my life, I need you so much. Please God, watch over my angel and bring her back to me well."

The girls and I sat in the waiting room for two hours. When the doctor finally came in to the room, he told us that during the angio Rose had suffered a full stroke. He spat out all kinds of medical terminology, but all I heard was stroke. I think I started to lunge for him, but the girls stepped in front of him and demanded to see their mother immediately. We, as a group, must have shaken him up a little because he moved back a bit and said that he'd like to explain her condition to us. "I have to see her right away. Right now," I shouted.

The doctor quietly said "You definitely have the right to see her right away. I would just like to explain what you should expect when you see her."

My heart was pounding and my body was in a cold sweat, and he wanted to explain what I should expect? "What, what should I expect? What have you done to her? All I want is to get her out of this place and to take her home. Now. I have to be with her. She needs me." I was ranting, and I knew it. But I was being smothered with fear and longing. Oh God. Why have you abandoned us? Why? Why? Rose doesn't deserve this. No, not my angel.

What the doctor told us was unbelievable. It was bad. Very bad.

My beautiful angel was paralyzed on her left side. She could not speak and she could not move. She would live, but she would need extensive, physical therapy. He said that her speech should return and that in time, she would be walking again. Now would be my time for patience and understanding. Of course, I would have done whatever it took to get my Rose well again. I wondered did he really think he had to tell me that? My angel was in the darkest time of her life, and I would do all that was in my power to bring her into the light again. I was nothing without her. With her, I could overcome anything. This was one setback that we would make right together. She was a fighter and by God, so was I.

When I entered her room, she was sleeping. Except for the tubes and the general hospital atmosphere, she looked as though she was sleeping peacefully in our bed at home. A nurse was standing beside her bed, checking Rose's vitals and the monitor, or whatever it was, kept up a nice steady beat. I sat down beside her and kissed her forehead. She seemed to stir for a moment but then fell back to sleep. I asked the nurse if she could tell our daughters where I was, and if they could come in to see their mother too. When the nurse left the room, I leaned over and kissed Rose's cheeks and whispered her name in her ear. There was no response and a sudden feeling of deja vous came over me. I had been here a long time ago only now it was my beloved wife before me, and not my mother. When the girls came in, they kissed Rose and whispered their love to her but she didn't move. We all just stood there staring at the love of our lives, and could not utter another word. We were terrified. We were not sure of what lie ahead for Rose, and it was consuming us with fear for her. What could you say when your heart is breaking, and you are faced with the unknown?

I stayed the night with my sweet angel. Several times she awoke and I explained what had happened, and how she would overcome this in time. The only recognition that she understood what I was saying, was a slight nod of her head, and tears streaming down her cheeks. I slipped into the chapel in the morning while the nurses were tending to her needs. I was frightened , heartbroken, and angry. I thought, if I lost Rose, it would have been the end of me. I could never live without her. I prayed and begged for my Rose to live. I tried bargaining with God to take me and let my angel live a normal life with our children and all of the grandchildren she loved dearly. I knew that for now, and for as long as I lived my primary concern would be for Rose. Whatever challenges lie ahead, I would fight them head on.

Chapter 72

Two weeks later, Rose was moved to another hospital for therapy. Thank God she had improved and was ready for her therapeutic sessions. She was able to talk, which would improve in time, and to use her left arm. Walking again was going to take time, but she would at least be mobile in a wheelchair for the time being. I had to get back to work, so my visits were held to evenings and weekends. Thankfully between our daughters and grandkids her days were filled with visitors. She hated her therapy and the food. She never really spoke of her dislikes because she was too thoughtful for that, but I could see the stress in her eyes. She actually gave me an argument when I told her I wouldn't be going to our grandson Joey's wedding so I could be with her. I had to promise her that I would go to the reception after she fell asleep. On the night of the wedding, she seemed to fall asleep very fast, so I went to the reception. Would my angel ever stop thinking of me before herself? What a glorious woman. My heart wasn't in it, but not going to the wedding might upset Rose, and that was the last thing I wanted for her.

The wedding was lovely, but very lonely for me. Everybody tried their best to put me at ease, but I longed for Rose. Joey asked me to play the bones and when I tried to resist, they practically dragged me onto the stage. For ten minutes I was lost in the comfort of the music, but when the

191

music ended I had to rush to my angels side. Rose was awake, as I'd suspected, and wanted to hear all about the kids and the wedding. As I was telling her bits and pieces, there was a commotion in the hallway. When we looked up, Joe and Agnes, still in their wedding apparel, were coming to see their grandma. The look on Rose's face said it all. She was smiling from ear to ear and her eyes were sparkling with tears of joy. This was what she lived for. The mutual love of family. This was the moment of recognition for her. Hope was renewed. I knew that she would gather her will to live in the same way she has cradled, and maintained the love she shared with her children. I thought, "Thank you God. Thank you Joey and Agnes. Thank you Rose."

Within four weeks, she walked through our front door at home. She still needed support and sometimes a wheelchair, but she was home at last. I couldn't be happier. Our life together had been renewed and we had overcome our test to endure. I thought, "Welcome home my love. Tonight as I hold you in my arms again: I'll see you in my dreams. And I always will."

Chapter 73

October came all too soon, and it was time for Bill and MaryRose's wedding. Rose insisted she was fit enough to go to the wedding. When she was all dressed in the gown she had bought so many months before, I couldn't stop staring at the beauty before me. My Rose was still the most beautiful woman I had ever seen, and at that moment, the happiest woman in the world. On that day Rose would shine like the angel she was.

We had decided to use the wheelchair because it was going to be a long day, and we didn't want to take the chance of her tripping on the gown. This was just a kind of not facing the truth, kind of talk between us. The wheelchair was a necessity after all, although she could use a walker, it was still very hard for her to get around without more support. But trooper that she was, nothing would keep her from another grandson's wedding this time. The wedding was a restorative for her. She beamed and glowed all day and into the evening. By the time we got home that night, we were both exhausted and hit the sack immediately. I thought, "Job well done my angel. You proved yourself as usual."

The year 1977 had been such a tumultuous one that when March of '78 came and went, it took me a while before I realized that I had turned sixty and there was no curse of the dreaded fifty-nine. If I had died at fifty-nine and it was God's way of curing Rose, it would have been just fine with me. Her life had always meant more to me than mine. I guess I was given a reprieve so that I could be there to help Rose regain her old self once more. She was coming along just great. Doreen and Al started a weekly card game with us and I made Rose a little cardholder. She enjoyed this time spent playing cards and forgetting all else. She was happy. We all were happy. The year was ending with good news from our grandson Joe. He and Agnes had a baby. Now we were great grandparents to, what else, another male in the family. His name was Joseph. I think the angels were sending all the boy babies to our family. But, it seemed that every time we were at our happiest that old demon death came knocking at our door.

Chapter 74

Our sister-in-law Inez called from California with some terrible news. She hadn't called sooner because Gene was in the hospital for phlebitis and nobody felt it was very serious. After losing both legs, he lingered for a day and then quite suddenly died. I thought, "Oh no, not Gene. He is my best friend on earth. My brother." I couldn't believe it. Inez said it was up to me of course, but she didn't think that Rose should be told just yet, while she was still recovering. Rose, oh dear God. Gene was everything to her. He was her brother, father, and confidante. How could I tell her that he was no longer with us? I couldn't. Not yet anyway. This was something I swore never to do to Rose. His death must remain a secret until she is completely better. I felt this news could have meant a setback for her. I thought, "Please forgive me my angel. Goodbye dear friend and beloved brother. I will never forget you, Gene. Never."

Another part of my being was lost forever. Why must the ones we hold so close to our hearts be taken away from us so soon? My only salvation was that they are needed someplace else because of all the good they had done here.

It was very hard for me and the rest of the family not to mention Gene in front of Rose. And then something started niggling at my brain. Since her stroke Rose had never mentioned her siblings or her friends or even our

195

grandchildren. The only time she showed any recognition is when any of them visited. It was like out of sight, out of mind. Why? Was I just putting more into it than necessary? Could it just be her inability to speak as clearly as usual? I would have to keep a closer eye on this matter, and if it continued I would speak to the doctor about it.

Chapter 75

A new year had begun, 1979, and I wanted to have a sixtieth birthday party for Rose. When family and friends arrived on the day of her party, Rose looked slightly apprehensive and complained of a headache. Not even halfway through the party she asked to go to bed. Something was very wrong. This was not like Rose. At the wedding she was happy and enjoyed the closeness of our family.

I decided to take Rose to the doctor for a checkup, and to have a chance for me to talk to him. The doctor said she was progressing as expected and she would continue to do so. He said that the headache could be a psychological way for her to avoid too much attention because of a lack of confidence in herself. He also said that she did have a slight memory loss, but I shouldn't worry about that. Not to worry? Was he kidding? Slight memory loss? Lack of confidence? How do I help her? Patience and perseverance, he told me. I thought that if that's what it takes, then that's what she'll get from me. I will never give up trying to bring my angel back to where she was before the stroke.

I chose to stop working and devoted my every waking moment to the love of my life. Retiring at sixty-one wasn't so bad. It felt great being with Rose twenty-four/seven. I kept her clean, clothed, and well fed. I tried to keep her involved in our family, the local news, and anything that would keep her mind focused. Once a week my son-in-law, Al, and myself went to the club for a little relaxation and a chance for me to jam with the band. Doreen kept Rose company and all was moving along smoothly.

Rose was getting around a little more and although her emotions were sometimes slightly amiss, most of our days together were content. Man was I trying, but no matter how hard I tried my angel was still not completely herself yet. Time. That will do it. Time, and now I have plenty of that for her.

Chapter 76

The years were just flying by though. It was already 1980, and we were still trying to get a hold on a happy future. I was almost at my wits end when I came up with a great idea. If I started making photo albums for each of our daughters, Rose and I could look at all the pictures and talk about the memories of them.

Our first project was to get all the pictures and catalog them for each daughter. What a job. It took up most of our day and that was good for Rose. Every single picture brought back a memory, if not for Rose, then I could remember for her. It was working. The pictures were bringing back all of our past, and we would talk about them as we sorted them out.

A picture of our only granddaughter Deirdre had me laughing so hard that Rose had to join in even though the memory of that picture wasn't as vivid for her. And so I reminded her. When Deirdre was only five years old, she had the biggest crush possible on Elvis Presley. When we decided to take Doreen and Al to Las Vegas with us, the first words out of Deirdre's mouth were, "Tell Elvis I love him and I want his autograph." I think she was really five going on sixteen. So we did go to see Elvis, and luckily for Deirdre, we got to see his last performance before he died, and we brought back a bunch of Elvis memorabilia for his littlest fan.

While rummaging through our photos, we found the last picture that had been taken of my father during his short stay with us. The memories of what a sweet and loving man he was suddenly turned to a memory of what happened to us after his death. There had been instances where the favorite rocker of papas' would start to rock during the afternoon despite there not even being a hint of a breeze in the air. We used to just laugh it off and say, "Hi Pop" as we passed it. Pictures were tilted or fell off the walls for no apparent reason, and our baby grandchildren would have conversations with their friend "Mikey," and tell us that he was in the hallway. Sometimes it gave us a chill, but for the most part we simply ignored it because none of the adults had ever seen or heard anything.

A few years after pop's death Michael and his wife Deanna came to live with us. Michael and Deanna were Denis' brother and sister-in-law. A great couple of kids. They lived in the apartment in our attic that had been previously shared by papa, Tony, and Phil. A short while after Deanna had found out that she was pregnant, she had a miscarriage. She had become very depressed over her loss, and would spend a lot of her time recuperating in bed. One afternoon while we were all at home, Deanna surprised us by coming downstairs for a visit with us. For the first time in weeks, she looked happy and finally at peace with the world. The first words out of her mouth left us dumb-founded. "Thank you for sending that lovely man up to see me. He sat at the foot of my bed, and when he started talking in that cute little accent of his, I was overwhelmed by his kindness. He told me to have faith in God and the Blessed Mother because my baby was with them, and I will see him one day when it will be my time to join him. He also said that there are three more babies waiting to be born to me and my husband in the next few years."

I asked her what this man looked like and did he say his name. She said he was a little man with black, wavy hair, and he wore a white shirt and black trousers. And then she said,

"He told me to be happy with my life and to share the love that was in this house. Although he was leaving now, all I had to do was say "Mikey I need you." and he would be there for me."

No. This was insane. I had never believed in UFOs, aliens, and especially ghosts. But how could Deanna have been so accurate in describing a man she had never known? I'm glad that whatever Deanna experienced helped her. I'd like to believe papa was with us.

Chapter 77

The pictures went on hold for a while after that memory.
I'd get back to it another day. Rose tired out easily after these
photo sessions any way so after putting her in for a nap I
started working on a garden. What brought on that idea? Sure,
thinking about papa reminded me of how he loved working
with the soil. Well, why not? I'd been working outdoors all my
life, so being out in the elements was a boost for me. I planted
some rose bushes and daffodils for my angel Rose, and even
some tomatoes and basil. I found myself enjoying the feel of
the earth, and the joy in watching my work grow. As the plants
started to grow, Rose would sit outside and watch me working
in the garden. She started calling me Farmer Joe. I loved seeing
her sitting in the sun. She looked as vibrant and beautiful as the
first time I'd seen her. My angel.

I'd still kept Gene's passing from Rose when I received
more shocking news from California. Rose's brother Paul had
been hospitalized, lost his legs, and died just as Gene had.
What the hell. Was this some kind of a family heredity thing
going on? I prayed not. These were two good men lost in
succession. They were two men that I'd known for the better
part of my life. These two men had become my brothers and
were now gone forever. Again, I had to keep another tragedy
from Rose. At that point in her life, I knew that she'd be better
off not knowing. But I had no one to share my sorrow with.

And that broke my heart. I wanted to cry out my sadness and be comforted by my love. I wanted to hold my angel in my arms and comfort her. I may never be able to tell her the truth about her brothers. I could only be grateful that she was still here with me, and that alone made me the luckiest man alive. The "man up there" works in mysterious ways. I cried, "Rest in peace my little brother. I will never forget you. And tell Gene that I will take care of and love your sister Rose for all eternity."

It was 1981, another year, and another time to pray for fresh beginnings and happier times. I couldn't complain. Rose and I were getting along just fine. Sometimes I missed work and the good times we used to have. But the main thing was that we were still "living" and "loving" each other and our still growing family. My only regret was that Rose never fully recovered. She never complained and she was always at my side. That meant more to me than anything else. I have had more than any man could ever hope for. I had a beautiful wife to cherish and love, and three lovely daughters who had made our family flourish with so many beautiful children, grandchildren, and great grandchildren. I knew that when I left this world, and that wouldn't be till I was ninety-nine, I would leave knowing that a part of me lives on in my family.

Chapter 78

It was time to go back to the photo albums that I'd never completed for my girls. I was just about finished with Doreen's, album when I came to a picture of her in one of her dance costumes. Oh what memories that brought back. Rose and I were going over all the great memories we had of Doreen, when I suddenly remembered one time in particular. Our little "Twinkle Toes," as Rose called her did something that made me think twice about her future. I knew she always wanted to dance, so I shouldn't have been so surprised when she did what she did so many years ago.

I was watching television on a nice, quiet Saturday afternoon when the doorbell rang. Standing at the door was a man I knew from the club that I worked in. He had his own club then so I assumed he was visiting me about the entertainment he might be looking for. He came in and when we sat down, he said that he had put out an ad for entertainers, singers, dancers etc., and guess who auditioned for the chorus line? He said. "Your daughter."

"My daughter? You must be mistaken." I said.

He replied, "When I heard her name I put two and two together, and figured it was your daughter. I thought it was odd that she wanted to work at my club when she could be working at yours, so I asked her how you were doing. I was holding the contract for her to sign. She really can dance. She told me that she had another audition and would come back to sign the papers. She never came back so I thought I'd come over to see if everything is all right. Out of respect for you and our friendship, I just wanted you to know that your daughter would be a highlight to my show."

I couldn't believe what I was hearing. When I told him she was only sixteen, and that in no way would I have her dancing in a chorus line, he almost hit the floor. To make a long story short, she didn't get the job and she and I had a long talk. I told her I was willing to set up a meeting with Hermes Pan at Carnegie Hall if she really wanted to dance professionally. She had applied for a modeling career at Barbizon and wanted to try that first.

Daughters. Holy cow! What next? I thought that, with three beauties, surrounded by today's ideas on feminine power and strengths, I didn't stand a chance. And this was just the beginning. I still had two more daughters who would be wanting to have it their way. Those were my thoughts at that time. Since then? The four women in my life took over. Every one of them had me wrapped around their little finger.

Those memories were really good for Rose. They brought back the sparkle in her eyes, and a warmth in her heart that I hadn't seen for a long time. She was happy again.

I had to admit that something more than the use of her legs and speech had changed her after the stroke. It was as if a part of her, the happy, loving, part of her had been pulled from her and scattered in the wind like fallen leaves. My angel was lacking the inner glow she had shared with everyone who knew her. Rose's eyes revealed a loneliness and despair that were never there before. I felt helpless. I wanted to do so much for her, but somehow I had failed my angel at the most crucial time of her life.

These moments of past happiness were fleeting and gone in a split second. But I continued to show her the pictures as I completed the first album. Whether it was a few hours of revelry or just a brief interlude, hearing her laughter set my heart at ease. She would come back to me again. I was certain of that.

Chapter 79

When I gave the first album to Doreen she was thrilled. She said Eileen and Marie would be so excited when they had theirs too. That made me feel like it was all worthwhile. I would start on Eileen's album right away. Rose and I began going through Eileen's photos. What memories. Leave it to me to bring up the wrong ones though. What might have been somewhat sad at the time was unbelievably funny to me now. I do not think Eileen would agree with my warped sense of humor, but I couldn't help myself.

Eileen had always been our precious, little, happy girl. She was never naughty, always pleasant, and a pleasure to us. So if ever she did something that was not too good she was a nervous wreck. I guess my attitude didn't help because although I had never hit or screamed at my girls, they seemed to be afraid of disappointing me in any way. We never had any major problems with Eileen, but one time I guess I went a little overboard and really came down on her. I was just exiting the parkway on my way home from work, and I was tired and hungry. I guess I was a little grumpy too when I spotted a young couple right to the side of the exit smooching. My first thought was "These kids today. If that was my daughter." Much to my chagrin, it was my daughter. Not being one to hold back on my anger, as I sped past them I shouted "I'll see you at home." As they looked at me in horror, I realized that the young man was Eileen's steady boyfriend Denis. In my mind that didn't make a difference to me. I just did not like kids kissing in public. When I got home and told Rose what I'd seen, she just laughed and said "Why, Mr. Bones, I guess you never did that at their age, did you?" Ok, she was right. I would apologize to Eileen for being so hasty in my judgment, but I would still have to let her know that I did not think that it was proper behavior for young girls.

As if things weren't bad enough, I put the frosting on the cake when Eileen came home. We were all sitting at the table about to have dinner, for which Eileen was late, when she came into the house. Jokingly, I said, "Well, our princess has arrived." I didn't think I was being nasty, but Eileen was so upset and so unsure of what to expect from me, that she peed her pants and ran out of the room howling in fear and embarrassment. Rose ran after her, and that night I had a talk with my little girl and we made up. I swore that night that come what may, I would never act like that again to any of my girls. That was years ago and now Rose and I were able to laugh about my past misdemeanors. When we came to Marie's pictures we would try to only remember the really good times. I said, "Yeah, but the best times were when the girls did something rash. They were always such great daughters, and that warmed our hearts, but when they were naughty they tickled us pink." I suppose my sense of humor was a little warped.

Rose took my hand and told me to remember all the wonderful things I'd done for our daughters. She said, " You were always there when they needed your love and advice. You lavished them with beautiful weddings, and they never wanted for material things like clothes and cars." I agreed with Rose that we had both given them all of those things, but that I could have been gentler with them. "Oh, shut up Peanuts, let's do some more picture finding." She called me Peanuts. She hadn't called me that since I was nine years old. This was my angel. She hadn't forgotten anything. I guessed that the photo albums were working like some kind of therapy. I thought,

"Thank you God." The weather was getting cooler so I had to put the pictures on hold for a few days while I tended to the garden. Al set up a phone system for me, so Rose could call me if she needed me while I was outdoors. The problem was that she never called me, and I couldn't imagine why I was tiring out so easily working the gardening. I felt like I could take a break but that wasn't like me. Maybe it was just a cold coming on. I thought, "What the heck, I never get sick. Forget about it."

Chapter 80

Before we knew it another year was knocking at the door. Rose didn't want to go out on New Years Eve. When I asked her if anything was wrong, she said "It would be nice if we spent the beginning of a new year with just the two of us for a change. I think that would be nice for once. We haven't been alone ever for New Years Eve." She was absolutely right. From our first year together till now, we had always celebrated with our families. If this was what she wanted, how could I give her any less?

So for the first time in forty-six years Rose and I were alone for New Years Eve. Rose had fallen asleep by 9:00 p.m., so I carried her to bed. When I laid her down I was surprised to find myself weakened by her light weight, and my heart strained against my chest.

I laid down beside her and fell into a sound sleep. My sleep was interrupted by a soft kiss on my lips. I opened my eyes to find Rose cuddled next to me caressing my cheek as she kissed me again. I touched her cheek and kissed away a teardrop. "What's wrong angel? Did I interrupt your sleep?"

"I love you peanuts. Please don't ever leave me. I would die without you."

"Dear, dear Rose. I could never leave you. I need you more than you could ever know."

She looked at the clock on the nightstand and said "Look a New Year is about to start."

It was just seconds before 12:00 a.m., 1982.

Seeing Rose so upset unnerved me. Was she feeling depressed about her condition? If so, I had to do more to cheer her up. I had procrastinated with the completion of the albums for our daughters. With the winter months keeping us in the house so much I thought that would be a good way to get Rose back in the happy groove again. We went full steam ahead sorting out pictures once more. But it wasn't working. Seeing all the family pictures seemed to further depress my angel. Maybe she was feeling confused and disoriented, because she made no comments when we came across pictures of her siblings. That still bothered me but I couldn't push her into remembering. Either she did remember, and didn't want to talk about them because she missed them, or she really felt no recognition of her past loves. Whatever the reason, we put off the albums again and played games instead.

I guess she was feeling that something was missing too, because she surprised me one afternoon during our game time. She said "You know Joe I feel like I'm holding you back from living."

"*You* keeping *me* from living?" I replied. "You are my life. I am living the life I have always dreamed of. You are and will always be the essence of my life."

Rose took my hand in hers and said, "This is not enough for you Joe. You need to be out there working and entertaining."

I kissed her deeply and said "Baby, I am finally retired. It was time for me to relax and be with my angel. I wouldn't want it any other way."

So that was it then. She was feeling like a burden to me. How could I prove to her that she was far from being anything but the love of my life, and I am the one who needs her? "You are stuck with me forever Rose. I need your love every day and night of my life. You complete me."

Chapter 81

I don't know if I was starting to get depressed too because I was really starting to feel more and more like an old man. I'd been falling asleep early and finding it hard to get out of bed in the morning. My body felt like I'd been hit with a ton of bricks. When I ate, I had agida. When I did any thing physical, I would have to take a few minutes to rest because my heart would start pounding in my chest. I was probably coming down with the winter blues or I needed a checkup. There just wasn't enough time to worry about myself because Rose came first. And then it happened.

Doreen and Al had come for a visit and the four of us were playing cards, when I felt a wave of nausea hit me and my arm was aching. Al took me aside and insisted we take a run to the emergency room at the hospital and get me examined right away. That scared me and Al, being a firefighter, said that if I didn't go with him he'd call his company for an ambulance. The last thing I needed was to scare Rose, so I agreed to go with him. I was starting to feel very weak and I didn't want Rose to see me in pain. I told Rose that Al and I were going to try and find an open pharmacy to get some medicine for my agida. I figured that it was just a little white lie and that Rose would understand. Besides, I was sure I wasn't sick.

When we got to the hospital Al told them I was having a heart attack and they rushed me right in. I told Al I wasn't having a heart attack, and he said that it was the fastest way to get immediate attention in an emergency room. Well, he had a point. I didn't want to be away from Rose for too long anyway. But when the doctor and nurses started hooking me up with all kinds of stick-ons and probed and poked, it was all I could do to stay calm. I just wanted to get out of there and go home. The doctor took one look at me and my EKG, and said I had better relax and settle down because I was having a heart attack. Relax, calm down. How does anyone do that when they are told they are having a heart attack? I forced myself to calm down until the doctor said he wanted to admit me for further testing. Oh no. Not me. There had to be something more the doctor could do to get me out of there. He said I would be leaving the hospital at my own risk, and he gave me the name of a cardiologist I had to see first thing in the morning. He said that he would set up an appointment for me himself, and pleaded with me not to put it off. So I left the hospital.

On the ride back home, I let Al have it with both barrels. "See what you did? Now, I have to see another doctor tomorrow. I can't do this to Rose."

Al just listened to my ranting and finally said, "You can't not do this. Think of Rose. I will be here first thing in the morning and go with you to the cardiologist."

So after laying awake in bed all night and holding on to Rose with all my might, Al and I went to the doctor's office in the morning. I saw the doctor, answered all his questions, and submitted myself to more testing. It took two hours to be told that my heart was giving out, my blood pressure was too high, and I had diabetes and emphysema. What else? When did all this happen? I thought, "Now how do I take care of Rose? What happens to her if I don't make it?"

The doctor said I could live a normal life if I took the medicines he prescribed, stopped smoking, ate healthy, and slowed down. The only doable one of his rules I could follow was to take the medications.

Words cannot express the anger I felt. Why now? Why now when Rose needed me so much? The fear in my heart was for Rose. There was just no way I could leave her alone. I thought to myself, "These doctors don't know me . They think I'm just some average Joe. Well, I'll show them. I will take care of myself, and stick around for a long time. Rose and I will grow old together. I am not ready to leave my angel."

This was going to be a more relaxing spring for me. We would just take one day at a time easily enjoying a respite from all anxieties. We owed it to each other to reflect on the love we had shared since childhood. This new doctor's thinking was a little extreme though. Now, he wanted me to have an oxygen tank on hand at all times. All right, do as the doctor says. I get it. So, Al brought over an oxygen tank for me, showed me how to use it, and made sure it was always full. Ok. I was accepting all of this change and I promised to act accordingly. But it was driving me crazy. For a guy who had never been sick a day in his life, and thrived on his physicality, this was a stretch. Rose was unbelievable. She never questioned my sudden relaxation, the doctor's visits, or even the oxygen. That was a kind of relief because I wouldn't have known how to explain it all any way. Her constant love for me had always been a mystery to me. Why me? How did I deserve such devotion? I was happy to feel that she wanted to keep me around for a long time. I intended to oblige her, and just to keep it possible I prayed for God to help keep me around for Rose. He and I must never abandon my lovely angel.

Chapter 82

Every day I was feeling better and better. Summer was fast approaching and having neglected my garden, I decided to clean it up before it got too hot outside. When I finally checked on my garden, it was a disaster. I had to start digging up everything and replant right away. It was no problem. I was sure I could handle a small job like that. However, there was a slight problem though. My daughters, their husbands, and our grandchildren were constantly coming over. I knew it was to make sure I was taking care of myself, but I was annoyed by their obvious lack of trust in me. They had even gone so far as to hire a maid service to clean the house. What they didn't know was that their efforts were a waste of time because as soon as the cleaning lady left, I cleaned up after her. I liked my house cleaned a certain way, and only Rose and I myself knew how that was. God bless them. I loved them more and more. So to make everybody happy, I did very little in the garden until I couldn't stand it any longer. By August, I had to do something.

On one of those hot, August, days I went out to the garden. It was a Friday and I knew that would be the best day to work on the garden. That was usually the one day when everyone was either working or involved with his or her own responsibilities. There I was digging, sweating, and feeling the hot sun and humidity bearing down on me, when Marie's husband Joe pulled up. Oh damn. Now he'll spread the word.

He said hello, picked up the shovel, and finished the gardening. I felt like a fool. Not because he helped me, but because I was trying to put one over on my family and myself. I think I was taught a good lesson on that day. I had to remember my responsibility to Rose and myself. Ok, It was another lesson learned. Joe probably saved my life that day. The only luxury I allowed myself were the Wednesday nights that I still went to the club.

Al always came with me and I didn't drink or smoke while there. I felt more at ease with him accompanying me because of his experience with CPR in the fire department and his knowledge of the oxygen I was using all the time. I went to enjoy the company of my friends, but mostly to jam with the band. I loved the music and the feel of the clappers in my hands. I was absorbed, body and soul, in the music, and it was like a lifeline leading me into a world of sound and unreality. For those few hours, I was not of this earth. After a while though, reality sunk in. My life was not there but beside my wife. Rose was my true reason for living. Music was a lift, but Rose was my ascension into the heavens.

There were so many times that I didn't want to go out and leave her, only to hear her tell me that she wanted me to have at least one night of my own kind of music. So my summer passed without any episodes of my heart, or Rose's handicap. We had weathered the worst and were living in our own little world of just the two of us. We were happy, content, and even more in love then ever. We were talking all the time of our days of youth, marriage, and parenthood. We bragged about our daughters and grandchildren, and the more we talked about our family the more I feared that she might ask about Gene or Paul. I broke into a sweat. She quickly changed the subject and said, "How are you feeling Joe?"

I looked at her in surprise, and said "Me? I'm fine."

My lady held my hand and said, "You can't kid a kidder, Mr. Bones. I know you're hiding something."

"Rose, it's just the heat. For the first time in my life it bothers me."

215

"Oh," she slyly uttered, "the heat. And the oxygen helps that?"

Wow. Rose hadn't been that cognizant since her stroke. Was this finally the break through I'd been praying for?

If it was, life for my angel was going to be better than ever before. I didn't care if she would still need a walker or wheelchair. As long as we could communicate and share our love that would be good enough for me. Anything she wanted, she wouldn't have to ask for, I'd have it there for her in a flash.

I scooped her into my arms and through my tears of joy. I smothered her with kisses. My sweet, sweet angel was back. Thank God. It was my dream come true. The rest of the day was pure bliss for me. We kissed and talked. We kissed and laughed. All day long and into the night we talked of the future. Where we would go and what we would do. The joys to come were waiting for us and we would consume them. Uppermost in Rose's heart was that we both stay healthy. She made me promise to take care of myself as well as I had been taking care of her. That was no problem. We had so much more to live for. Nothing would stop us ever again.

That day had been one of the happiest days of my life. We had lived through so many good times but this was different because it opened a doorway to the future. We were going to be all right. Our love would endure. As we slept in each other's arms, I felt all of our problems dissolve. I thought to myself, " Good night my love. I'll see you in my dreams." And I did.

Chapter 83

The next morning I woke up at 5:30 as usual. This day I started with a heart full of joy and gratitude. My angel was with me once more. I wanted to have breakfast ready for Rose and the house straightened out before she woke up. What a special day I wanted it to be. Just as I had finished, the little bell I'd left at her bedside began to ring. "That's my girl," I thought, "she just wanted to make sure I was still around." I was on my way. As I entered the bedroom I couldn't believe what I was seeing.

Rose was struggling to sit up and that look had come back to her eyes. How can I explain that look? It was as though she just wasn't completely there. It was a look of confusion and the indifference was back. Dear God, Why? Just the previous day she was my Rose, but today she was, just different. I rushed to her side and helped her to sit up.

"Are you ready for breakfast, Rosie?" She looked at me as if she had just seen a stranger.

"My head hurts. I need my medicine."

I was crushed. Eventually, she came around again. It wasn't like the previous night, but it was the usual. Maybe it was just a minor setback. Only time and patience would tell, and I had plenty of that.

By the time Wednesday night came around nothing had really changed. She had gone into a fog of retreat and there was nothing I could do about it. I thought about going to the club with Al and so I gave him a call. He always came with me, but for the first time he begged off. The kid wasn't feeling well himself and asked if we could make it the following week instead. I knew how he must have been feeling because I wasn't feeling great either. It was probably the change in the weather. September always goes from one extreme to another. It would be hot one day, and cool the next. I called it Flu weather. He came over anyway to talk me out of going, and I saw how sick he looked. I explained that I would be fine, all the regular guys would be there, and they always watched me like hawks. Before he left he insisted on making sure that the oxygen tank was filled and placed it in the trunk of my car. With that taken care of, he said goodnight, and asked me to call him if I didn't feel well. I agreed and sent him home. Marie came to our house about nine o'clock to stay with her mother and I put Rose to bed. When I tucked her in, she put her arms around me and kissed me goodnight. That was a good sign. So I kissed her again and said "Pleasant dreams baby. I'll see you in my dreams." She countered with "No, I'll see you in my dreams first." God how she made me feel so good. I absolutely adore my angel.

It was a slow night at the club, so we were able to start jamming right away. For old times sake, the guys played "Sweet Georgia Brown" for me and I whipped those bones into a frenzy. I was having a great time when I started feeling a little woozy. The guys dropped everything and sat me down right away. I told them I had an oxygen tank in the car and one of them ran out to get it. He came running back real fast, but by that time I was laying on the floor and the guys were calling for an ambulance. As they were trying to give me the oxygen I overheard one of them say that he thought the tank was empty. I knew it wasn't, but I just didn't have the strength to do it myself. I guess I started to panic because I felt my heart go crazy, and I must have passed out. My last thought before going dark was "Rose, angel I'm sorry."

Chapter 84

What happened? Where am I? I feel really weird, I was thinking. I hear voices all around me. I can't make out who's talking and I can't seem to say anything to them. Oh no, did I have a stroke? I can't move either. I'm trying to move, to talk, anything. Is this how my angel felt when she had her stroke? Hey, listen up everybody. I can hear you and I've been trying to answer you. I don't understand why you can't hear me, and why I can't see you. Am I blind too? Rose, Rose baby. Are you there? I don't know what's going on. I just know that I'm very tired. Maybe I'll sleep awhile. That's better.

Wow, I must have fallen asleep really fast because I'm dreaming already. I just walked into our apartment and there's Rosie. Boy is she gorgeous. Where's she going? Rose just slipped into another room and I'm following her. Yep, there she is with our three little girls. What beautiful babies we have. Hey, they just got up and ran into another room. I have to follow them. There they are, all grown up and as beautiful as their mother. What's wrong? They're crying. I can feel their tears on my cheeks as they kiss me. Don't cry my little angels. Daddy's right here for you. I will always be here for you.

Whoa, the room is spinning. I'm spinning. I don't feel dizzy though because I catch glimpses of people standing around me. Holy mackerel, it's like a kaleidoscope. Look it's mama and there's papa right beside her, and I can't believe it

219

but there's Sam right next to them. They are all smiling and they look so happy to see me. They are saying something, but I can't hear what it is. Hey Sam. Hey brother. He's waving to me and pointing to his side. My God, it's mama Anna with Gene and Paul. Hey, I love you all and boy have I missed you. But hold on I feel myself being pulled somewhere else. I'm alone again. It felt so good seeing everybody and knowing that they could see me too. Wait till I tell Rose. She won't believe it. One thing is for sure. I'm the luckiest man in the world. I have known so much love and to think I shared the greatest love of all with that littlest, most beautiful of angels ever since that wonderful day in September a lifetime ago.

I can still feel the cool breeze of that night when I left the feast thinking I'd never see that angel again. I never did understand how I could have been so smitten with the beauty of that little girl, when I myself was so young. But she was etched into my heart and I was so sad at never having the chance to see her again. And to think that I would see her once more so many years later. I have always felt that we were destined to be together forever. She was the only certainty in my life. Our love has been my strength. Now, I feel as if I am being pulled away from my angel. I must wake up. This restless sleep I'm having is insane. It's not right. How can I sleep when I know she needs me?

If only those voices would stop calling me. What do they want? Don't they know I have to take care of Rose? Please leave me alone. I don't want to be here. I must go home. Yes, home. Our place of refuge. Rose and I together. We have had enough separations that tried our love. Nothing has ever kept us apart for long. First, it was the orphanage. The torment there wasn't half as bad as not being able to be with Rose.

We had just started on the road to an everlasting friendship and maybe more, when I was torn away from her. The desperation and loss I had felt during all those years were finally gone on the night we found each other again. I can still see in my heart of hearts how beautiful she looked in the glow of the moonlight that night. Her lovely hair falling over her shoulders, her sparkling white teeth glistening as she smiled, the softness of her voice as we spoke of our times apart, and most of all, the love in her eyes. We were together at last and our journey through life had begun.

As fate would have it, we were pulled apart once again. This time it was because the world had started to fall apart. World War II took me away from my angel this time. Our love was put to the test again. But nothing could take that away from us. Our love sustained and grew through four years of uncertainty. Would she and our baby girl be safe at home? Would I ever get back to them alive and in one piece?

Well, I did, and they were both there waiting for me. We were so blessed. Our love was enriched for thirty more years. Rose gave me two more sweet daughters to love. We had no more separations, and we were always together and living the best years of our lives, that is, until the day of her stroke. We weren't physically apart, but Rose was emotionally struggling to regain her true self. Nothing changed for me. She was still my one and only angel of love. I understood her despair and I tried to convince her that she could never be less than what she'd always been, which is the most beautiful, loving, and caring woman that I and everyone who is a part of her adores. It has been five years since her stroke and my only regret is that I haven't been able to make her see how much she is loved. Sometimes I lay awake at night wondering if it's my fault that she became so ill.

I remember all the years she insisted on working and that pains me to think if that might have had something to do with her condition. She always insisted that she enjoyed being a working woman. But did not being with her daughters all the time put a strain on her? I often asked her if she'd rather not work, yet she continued and seemed content. I would never force her not to do anything that she wanted to do. Maybe I should have. I don't know. She did quit on her own though when Marie was born. And even then it seemed to me that she regretted her decision not to work. She made my head spin with indecision. I should've, could've. I never had the right answers. It has to be my fault.

When I wake up, the first thing I'll do is tell her how important she is to me and the girls. Then I will beg her forgiveness for not having been there for her needs. That's it. Rose was always thinking about everyone else but herself. I should have picked up on that sooner. Well, now is the time to get moving. Come on Joe, wake up.

What is wrong with me? I can't get away from those voices in my head. Who are you and what do you want? There's mama and papa again. What are you saying? I can't hear you. They are holding out their hands to me. I want to touch them, but I can't seem to move. No, I don't want to go to them. I have to get back to Rose.

Let's see if I can start putting things together. Why am I feeling so exhausted? I am not in pain, just tired. Why am I so tired? I know something must have happened to me because I can't move and I can't open my eyes. Oh my God. Was I in a car accident or something? Maybe that's it. I had a car accident after leaving the club, and now I'm paralyzed. After leaving the club? I don't remember that. I sure wasn't drinking so why don't I remember being on my way home?

I do remember jamming with the band though. We were really going at it. I played the clappers to "Sweet Georgia Brown" and then I sat at the drums for some heavy jazz. We were in a groove. The music was hot. No wait a minute. I was hot. I must have been sweating up a storm. Yeah, I remember feeling the sweat on my brow and it pouring down my back. Then my arm started tingling and I felt a little woozy. I couldn't stop playing though because we were right in the middle of "Flight of the Bumble Bee." Yeah, I remember that all right.

I'm really racking my brain trying to figure this one out. What else was going on? I can't get a grasp on it. Up to that moment everything is clear to me. Then what happened? Everything is pretty fuzzy after that. I do remember sitting in a chair. No, I was on the floor. No, that can't be. Wait a minute, wait a minute. I remember floating in the air, no someone was carrying me. Noise was all around me. Sounds like sirens.

Hey that must be it. I had an accident and was in an ambulance. But why can't I remember anything else? Oh, this is too much for me. I'm getting exhausted trying to put it all together. I have to rest and get some more sleep.

Chapter 85

The minute I try to sleep I find myself in a void with people all around me. They look so familiar. Hey, Gene is that you? What's going on? He just smiles and points to something ahead of me. What is that? I can't make it out. It's so bright. I'm so tired. So very tired. Something is tugging at me. I feel the need and the thrill of fulfillment, pulling at me. I must rest, sleep, and let go. But my heart is telling me not to let go. I must stay for Rose. She needs me. I can't let go.

There are the voices in my head again. This is like a family reunion. Everybody is here to see me. There's mama, papa, Sam, mama Anna, Gene, and Paul. There are even some of the guys who didn't make it home from Guam. But how can that be possible? Have I been lost in a dream and none of these people have been gone from my life? They are calling me, but I can only think of Rose right now. My sweet angel Rose.

Oh, here she is. I hear her loving voice. She's here. Right beside me. Holding my hand and whispering in my ear. I want to look into her big, blue eyes and tell her how much I love her. I want to hold her in my arms and kiss her soft lips. I want to see my lovely girls and hold them too. But I just cannot move or speak. I am trying my four angels. Believe me I am trying very hard to talk to all of you. It's just not

224

happening. I want to be close to you and love you forever. I just can't. Please forgive me.

Rose, I hear you baby. I feel your hands on mine. I feel your soft lips kissing me. Now, your lips are on my ear and I hear you whisper.

"Joe. It's time for you to rest now. I will always love you, Joe. We know our love is forever. You have been my hero and protector long enough. Rest now Mr. Bones, dear heart. Remember this prayer we shared so many times."

"When you feel a touch on your cheek,
that will be me kissing you,
When you feel a touch on your shoulder,
that will be me protecting you,
When you hear the wind in the trees,
that will be me whispering to you,
I will always be with you,
My love for you is too strong not to hold on to you."
"I'll see you in my dreams my love."

Oh, that voice. I do remember angel, I will always remember our special prayer and the depth of our love. Rose, you helped me define and realize the meaning of "living" and "loving." You gave me hope when I thought there was none. You gave me love when I thought I had been forsaken. You put the joy of life in me when I had no conception of what life was really all about. Thank you sweet angel. You enriched my soul.

I can feel the warmth of your breath on my face and your soft kiss on my lips. Yes, I will rest now, knowing that we have a love that will last forever. The power of her love overtakes me. Goodnight my angel Rose, goodnight.

I'll see you in my dreams 'till we are together again.

Chapter 86

On September 21, 1982, fifty-five years after finding his angel, Joe Bones slipped away peacefully. He was sixty-four years old. He never awoke from his coma.

Almost exactly thirteen months later, on October 16, 1983, his beloved angel, Rose, succumbed to cancer. She was sixty-four years old.

Not even death could keep them apart. Their legacy of love lives on in their children and their children's children and will continue to grow for all eternity.

This is a story that has no ending.

Printed in the United States
131485LV00003B/16-18/P